# Romancing Lord Ramsbury

Brides of Brighton Book 3

ASHTYN NEWBOLD

Copyright © 2019 by Ashtyn Newbold
All rights reserved.

No part of this book may be reproduced in any form whatsoever, whether by graphic, visual, electronic, film, microfilm, tape recording, or any other means, without prior written permission of the publisher, except in the case of brief passages embodied in critical reviews and articles.

This is a work of fiction. The characters, names, incidents, places and dialogue are products of the author's imaginations and are not to be construed as real. Any resemblance of characters to any person, living or dead, is purely coincidental.

ISBN 13: 9781075439841

Editing by Tori MacArthur

Front cover design by Blue Water Books

*For Payton, the best sister ever.*

# Chapter 1

BRIGHTON, ENGLAND, SPRING 1814

Looking up from the pages of her novel required great self-discipline, a quality which Grace Weston had always claimed with pride.

But self-discipline was also a quality that her sister desperately lacked.

Collapsing on the grass with frustration, Grace's elder sister Harriett scowled, the expression reminding Grace of another moment, just days before, when her sister had returned from town with yet another bag of purchases. Harriett's honey-blonde curls flew back from her face as she blew out a puff of air, tossing aside her new parasol. "Why must the shops be so alluring, Grace?" She stroked the brim of her new bonnet which she wore, the blue ribbons twisting with the breeze.

Grace shrugged, studying her sister. "The bonnet is

very becoming. The blue does much to complement the color of your eyes."

With a sigh, Harriett tucked her legs under her. "Yes, but it is the third bonnet I have purchased this month, and with the parasol, all my pin money is spent."

"And it is only the fifth of April." Grace tried to hide her smirk, but Harriett saw it.

"You take pleasure in my suffering," Harriett said with narrowed eyes. "I have a genuine addiction to the Brighton shops. Mama said I would grow out of it, but each time I venture to town there are new creations in the windows to tempt me. And our pin money has been decreasing each month." She chewed her lip. "Have you noticed?"

"You might consider avoiding the shops altogether," Grace said thoughtfully. "Then you shall not be so tempted."

"But I have very few pastimes I enjoy so much as shopping." Harriett gave a dramatic groan.

Grace licked the tip of her finger, turning the page of her book. The story had almost taken her to a romantic proposal, and she had been eager to discover the heroine's response.

"Please pay attention," Harriett said in an irritated voice.

Grace raised her eyes, meeting her sister's blue ones with a scowl. "I believe it was you who first interrupted me."

"That is true, but this is more important than a silly novel."

Grace snapped the book shut. "A novel is much more important than discussing your hundredth bonnet."

Harriett touched her new piece of headwear, indignation spreading over her features. "One can never have too many bonnets."

"One can never have too many books."

With one eyebrow raised, Harriett shook her head.

"Only if she hopes to be deemed an unmarriageable bluestocking."

Grace bit back the harsh retort that hovered on her tongue. It was impossible for her not to rise in defense when her reading habits were questioned. Yes, she loved books, but why was it deemed a less worthy pastime than obsessing over headpieces and parasols? Or stitching a boring piece of embroidery? Why should it make her unmarriageable?

Grace took great care in studying the heroes of the novels she read, taking note of their agreeable qualities, determining which she would seek in a husband. She enjoyed reading romantic stories and poetry the most, which would serve her well in a courtship. But whenever she tried to convince her mother, or even her sister, of the merits of reading novels, they simply did not understand.

She blamed their poor sense on a lack of the very thing they censured her for. Reading.

Her mother claimed Grace would never marry, as she seemed to prefer fictional men over real ones. But her mother never seemed to worry over Harriett, even though she was the eldest, unmarried at the age of twenty-one. If either daughter were in danger of spinsterhood it was Harriett.

And so Grace's own marriage wasn't her primary concern. Eventually she would give it greater thought, but she was the younger daughter. As a benefit to her constant reading of romantic stories, and the observations she had made of her own parents, she had learned what made two people well-suited to one another. She enjoyed making matches in her mind of the residents of Brighton—yet another of her pastimes that was frowned upon.

She had the perfect match in mind for her sister.

If only Harriett would listen.

Grace exercised her self-discipline once again, setting her book far away on the grass. "If I am to be an unmarriageable bluestocking, then you are to be an unmarriageable shopper. If you continue on in this way you will not be able to marry Mr. William Harrison."

Harriett's eyes rolled back in annoyance as she leaned on her hands. "Will you please stop with your attempts to match me with him?"

"I cannot. To do so would be abandoning hope for your future happiness." Grace sighed as she stared at the branches above her. "I do wish for you to be happy. William always made you smile."

As children, Mr. Harrison had often played on the beach with Harriett and Grace. It had not escaped Grace's keen notice that he fancied her sister. But one day Harriett had stopped coming to the beach, stopped having an imagination, and shut herself away to decorate hats and stitch embroidery. The memory of the imaginary games they played, the joyful friendship they all had shared, filled Grace with melancholy. Harriett had claimed that it was time for her to grow up and prepare herself for a match of esteem. Grace suspected Harriett had developed feelings for their friend, feelings she knew would lead her away from her dreams of wealth and prestige.

But Grace had not given up hope for the match. There was much to recommend it. William dressed in a modest fashion, a needed contrast to Harriett's extravagant style. He possessed a fine intellect and valued literature, which Grace hoped would transfer to her sister. Humble and genuine, with a friendly disposition, he would serve well to reduce Harriett's often extreme temperament. His only fault was that he was not in possession of a large fortune, a needed quality in Harriett's husband if she did not overcome her addiction to purchasing new accessories.

A sadness entered Harriett's eyes, perhaps a yearning for those days that Grace had just recalled in her own mind. But Harriett quickly shook it away, an accusatory look replacing it. "You speak of him so much, I would suspect you fancy him yourself."

"I do not." Grace laughed under her breath. The idea was ridiculous. Mr. Harrison was the perfect match for Harriett, not herself. "Besides, I'm not well suited to him like you are."

"I'm not well suited to him! You know how I have always dreamed of managing a large estate and obtaining a title. And to be called *Harriett Harrison*?" She grimaced, smoothing her palm over the grass.

Grace laughed. "What's in a name? That which we call a rose by any other name would smell as sweet."

Harriett frowned. "Who said that?"

"Shakespeare!" Grace tried to hide her dismay, but couldn't. How could her sister not recognize such famous words? Grace could argue that even Romeo Montague and Juliet Capulet were less compatible than her sister and Mr. Harrison.

Harriett's scowl deepened. "In any case, I disagree that Mr. Harrison and I are well suited to one another. I have known him since I was a small child, and I have never sensed that he holds any attachment to me. And how would he be able to provide me with the pin money that my happiness so depends on? He is not wealthy." Her voice carried a hint of teasing, but Grace sensed truth behind her words.

"His attachment to you is clear; I would venture to call you blind to have missed it." Grace widened her eyes to emphasize her words. "William is well established in his profession as a barrister, so there is no reason that you should not have a comfortable living. At any rate, wealthy men are all so scoundrelous and arrogant." Grace's upper lip curled with distaste. "I dislike the lot of them. You should not sacrifice a good man for one of wealth and title."

Harriett raised a finger in accusation. "You cannot say that of *all* wealthy men. The only man of wealth I know to fit that description is Lord Ramsbury."

Grace's heart stirred with anger at the mere mention of the man's name. *Lord Ramsbury*. Scoundrelous and arrogant did not even begin to describe him, and the word *dislike* could not describe her distaste for him. As the eldest son of the Earl of Coventry, Lord Ramsbury was the most desirable bachelor in all of Brighton. He flaunted his wealth and status in the public eye, and his reputation for outrageous flirting had certainly spread through the bulk of England.

He was adored by society because he was handsome, charming, and would soon be inheriting his father's earldom. Women flocked to him, yet he was notorious for turning them away. But not before stealing their hearts with an array of insincere flattery and other disreputable things.

But these reasons were small factors, small annoyances contributing to Grace's distaste for the man. She had been despising Lord Ramsbury for almost as long as he had been shamelessly flirting with women, which was a long while indeed.

Three years before at her first ball, he had been there. All her romantic heart had seen were his striking blue eyes, athletic figure, and deep golden hair. He had sought her out at her place against the wall, offering a string of flattery that she had believed. Three dances later, and she had considered herself to be madly in love with him. Three dances, after all, signaled to the party an interest of courtship, of marriage. She could scarcely believe that Lord Ramsbury had chosen to pursue her. Foolish as she was, she had spent the next four months thinking of him constantly, pining for him.

Until the next ball, when he had forgotten her name.

Grace shook herself of the dreadful memory. She preferred to think of pleasant things.

"I hope Lord Ramsbury finds himself beneath the wheels of a carriage," Grace mused, tapping her chin with one finger. "Or under the hooves of a stallion."

Harriett gasped, dismay contorting her pretty features. With a grin, Grace reached for her book again.

Her sister lunged forward on the grass, slapping Grace's hand away, recalling her eyes. "Why do you hate Lord Ramsbury so very much?"

Grace pursed her lips in annoyance, abandoning her book once more. "I will answer you that if you explain to me why you stopped coming to the beach when we were children. Why did you stop being William's friend?" Grace had always wondered what had brought about such an abrupt change in her sister. Harriett had been at the beach with Grace, William, and their friend, Rose Daventry, playing joyfully like any other day, and the next she had remained at home. Grace had found her inside with her bonnet strings pulled tight, expressing a rigid disapproval of their games. She refused to ever venture to the ocean, and grew tense at every mention of William Harrison.

Harriett's expression closed off, leaving her emotions

to flounder inside. "I realized how dangerous it was. The ocean, such close friendship with a boy… we were growing older. It was no longer proper."

"Twelve is not so very old."

"William was fourteen."

Grace closed her lips against further questioning. She had received the same vague answer for years. The romantic within her clung to hope that one day Harriett and William would come together again, but it was a distant hope indeed if Harriett refused to speak to him.

Grace released a dramatic sigh, one she reserved only for talk of unscrupulous men. "You already know why I despise Lord Ramsbury. Need I endure the torture of relaying it again? He spurned me, Harriett. He told me I was the most beautiful girl he had ever beheld. He compared my eyes to the night sky, and my hair to a bronze picture frame, as it 'outlined the beauty of my unrivaled features.' And then he tossed me aside like a sullied napkin. He is odious and egotistical and… infuriating. How dare he toy with a young girl's heart in such a way? And I am not the only one he has fooled."

Harriett scoffed, apparently unsatisfied. It bothered Grace that men of wealth and title received a closer examination of their character—a determined search for any sign of honor—while men of lower station were scrutinized from the condition of their gloves to the alignment of their teeth. Grace did not require that her husband be wealthy, although she was certainly not opposed to it. But from her experience in society, she had observed that the men most lacking in character seemed to be the least lacking in wealth. It inspired arrogance and superiority, which Grace could not stand in the least.

Harriett pressed the subject further. "Surely Lord Ramsbury has a redeeming quality or two. A person cannot be entirely bad."

"He may be the exception," Grace grumbled.

Her sister looked up at the clouds, deep thought evident in her features. "I can think of many redeeming qualities he possesses."

Grace raised an eyebrow in doubt.

"His firm jaw, his blue eyes, and his devilish smile to begin."

It was Grace's turn to scoff. "May we speak of something else? Or rather, *someone* else? She gave a wide smile. "William Harrison. If you would only make an effort to reacquaint yourself with his character, then you would see how perfectly designed you are for one another."

Harriett cast her eyes heavenward. "Your romantic notions are too much."

"And yours are not enough."

Harriett pinched her lips together before speaking. "I am not interested in Mr. Harrison."

"But I suspect he is interested in you, and he always has been."

"What has led you to that conclusion?"

Grace shrugged, rolling a blade of grass between her fingers. "I have a sense for things like this. For… things involving the heart."

"You act as if you are an expert in love." Harriett waved her hands in the air in a dramatic fashion. "As if you are Aphrodite herself."

"Perhaps I am an expert. My reading has taught me much on the subject. Please say you'll consider it."

"Consider what, exactly?"

Grace flashed a bright smile. "Courting Mr. Harrison."

"He has not made any indication that he wishes to court me!"

"I suspect it's because he is afraid. He doesn't know if you'll accept him. You must encourage him into a courtship. Charm him, flirt with him."

"I'm certainly not going to encourage such a thing." Harriett stood from the grass in one swift motion, setting off toward the house. "And I don't wish to discuss it any longer."

Grace threw her book onto the grass, jumping to her feet. She tripped over her skirts as she hurried after her sister. "Please! It would be so delightful if you did marry him."

Harriett turned around, her brow furrowed. "Why? Only so you can prove you are this 'expert in love?'"

As Grace puzzled over it, she found some truth behind her sister's words. So many young ladies engaged their time in sociality, flirting, and pursuing the men of their choice. Grace wanted a way to prove to her own family that her reading was not a waste of time. She was learning many things that would help her one day catch a husband. In fact, she was fully confident that she could catch one if she set her mind to it. And she could help her sister secure the perfect husband for herself, using her own knowledge and expertise.

Grace stopped, planting her hands on her hips. "Perhaps I am an expert. You can become a master on any subject by reading extensively on it."

"But experiencing it in reality would provide much greater enlightenment."

"Not always." Grace smiled. "And it is hardly proper to seek out experience in romance, is it? Unless you mean that you will try it by romancing Mr. Harrison. I would approve of that venture."

Harriett huffed a breath. "I would rather see *you* try."

"Me?"

Harriett's eyes grew wide, an idea growing within them. Her lips pursed in a smirk. "I would like to see you try to woo Mr. Harrison. If you can manage to catch his attention, I will believe that you are this expert you boast of being."

Grace shook her head hard. "No. That would be detrimental to my plan for Mr. Harrison's match with you."

Harriett shrugged one shoulder, the motion scrunching the fabric of her layered blue sleeve. "I knew you were not capable of it."

Irritation welled up inside Grace, her entire body tightening. "I most certainly am. But I simply refuse to romance Mr. Harrison. He is yours."

Harriett gritted her teeth. "He is not mine."

"One day he will be."

"Grace!" Harriett released a long breath through her nostrils, straightening her posture. "Very well, if you will not accept my challenge, then I extend a different one. After all, wooing Mr. Harrison would be all too easy for an *expert*."

Grace's heart pounded in anticipation, and her feet bounced within her slippers. She never could resist a challenge. "What is it?"

Her sister pressed her lips together, amusement striking her eyes. "Let us make it a wager."

"A wager? I don't think Papa would approve." Grace strived to please her parents, to always respect their wishes. Her father rarely noticed her efforts, but she extended them all the same. The only wish of her mother that Grace remotely rebelled against was her reading habits. How could she abandon the stories that thrilled and enlightened and so thoroughly entertained her? She chewed on her lower lip in hesitation.

"Papa will not know of our wager." Harriett's eyebrow lifted along with her mischievous smile.

Grace fidgeted with the lace of her skirts. "You must tell me what it is before I will agree to it." She did not like the devious twinkle in her sister's eye.

"Lord Ramsbury," Harriett said.

The name crawled over Grace's skin, deepening her scowl. "What of him?"

Her sister leaned forward, lowering her voice. "If you can manage to woo Lord Ramsbury into a proposal, I will believe you are indeed an expert in love, and I will trust your counsel to court Mr. Harrison."

Grace gasped, pulling away. "I would never marry Lord Ramsbury!"

"I did not say you had to *marry* him, only coerce him into a proposal." Harriett's smile, broad and wicked, showed that she felt the odds were in her favor. "No doubt he has dozens of women seeking his hand. It would indeed require an expert to catch his eye."

The idea sat heavy and sharp in Grace's stomach, filling her with dread. She could never face Lord Ramsbury again. And she could certainly not *romance* him.

"If you are successful," Harriett said, "I will surrender all my pin money to you for the next three months, and agree to court Mr. Harrison. I will even declare to Mama that your reading should be condoned, giving you full responsibility for the match. But if you fail, you will give me your pin money and never mention Mr. Harrison again."

Grace narrowed her eyes. "I see you have great confidence in me. You would never offer your own pin money if you had even the slightest fear of losing it."

Harriett gave a loud laugh.

Grace's breath came quickly, catching in her chest like fire. She had never put into practice the advice she so readily gave to her sister. How could she succeed? Why would a man like Lord Ramsbury pay her any notice? He had once before, but it had been a game, a trap. He had used her young heart like a plaything, cruel and unforgiving.

A thought struck her. But if she could manage to win his proposal, she could have the pleasure of offering him the rejection he unwittingly gave her three years before.

A slow smile touched Grace's lips. Aside from being well-read on the subject of courtship and romance, she was also well-read on the subject of revenge.

"Do you agree to the terms?" Harriett stepped forward, propping her parasol over one shoulder.

"Not quite." Grace's mind spun. "This is a great feat you ask of me. Your return must be equal and fair. In your courtship with William, you must agree to a minimum of three meetings with him, should his attachment extend that far, which I believe it shall."

Harriett considered it for the briefest moment. It seemed she wasn't worried at all that she might lose. "Very well. Three."

Extending her hand, Grace gave her sister a confident smile, though she didn't feel it. "I believe this is what men of business do when sealing a bargain."

Harriett gave Grace's hand a quick shake, grinning in premature triumph. Grace hoped her sister couldn't feel how much her hand shook.

What had she done?

"Hmm," Harriett mused as they walked toward the back door of the house. "What shall I buy with my abundance of pin money? A new pair of slippers? Perhaps a new shawl or ballgown?"

"It would be unwise to already plan your purchases." Grace squared her shoulders, willing herself to appear confident.

But inside she was quite the opposite.

The very thought of approaching Lord Ramsbury had her stomach in knots. But she had never been one to countenance the act of giving up. She liked a challenge, and she didn't appreciate her abilities being doubted. Her insides writhed and twisted like a den of snakes, constricting her lungs until she couldn't breathe. There had been something about Harriett's smirk that had led Grace to agree so hastily to the wager.

"You do realize that in order to woo Lord Ramsbury you will have to pretend to like him." Harriett giggled, turning her face away from the house. "To do so will feed his arrogance. I expect you will surrender your efforts the moment you begin, for how will you tolerate flattering him?"

Grace bit her lip, squeezing her eyes shut in regret. When she opened them, she found Harriett facing her once again, her face shrouded in sunlight. For a moment she looked angelic, a halo of light surrounding her pale hair and ivory dress. But her smirk contradicted the picture.

With a resolute tone, Grace said, "I will tolerate it because I know that when he does propose, I will have the privilege of denying him." She felt the memory of those four hopeful months, three years ago, when she had fancied herself in love with him. She had been certain he had returned her affection, and that he would soon call upon her to begin their courtship.

Then came his careless hands, snapping her young heart into fragments.

"Lord Ramsbury has broken many hearts and rejected many women," Grace continued, "yet I severely doubt he has experienced the same. How could he have? Perhaps if he learns how it feels he will be more careful."

Harriett's giggling did not lessen for a moment. She pressed one hand to her stomach, tears pooling in her eyes.

"What is so humorous?" Grace snapped.

"I'm imagining you attempting to flatter Lord Ramsbury." She swiped at her lashes, picking up the moisture there as she laughed. Harriett's imaginings came rarely, and when they did, they were often of disagreeable things.

"I suspect you will be offering *me* no such flattery." Grace let out a long puff of air, tipping her neck in a circle to stretch it. She shook her arms at her sides, trying to gather a bit of fortitude.

"Shall we try to find him now?" Harriet asked. "I assume he will be in the assembly rooms. I have not visited for months, but when I did, he seemed as if he spent the majority of his life there."

Grace gave her sister a look of dismay. "We mustn't go now. I have not had time to prepare."

"There is no better time. An expert would not require intense preparation."

Fear tightened in Grace's chest, her pride flaring. What had she been thinking? She couldn't do this. Lord Ramsbury would simply toss her aside all over again before she had a chance to try. Harriett would win, and Grace would be penniless for three months.

*Harriett would win.*

If there was anything Grace could not tolerate it was that.

"Very well. We shall go this very instant," she said, regretting the words the moment they passed her lips.

Harriett clapped her hands, a bright smile spreading over her mouth. "I'll fetch my pink bonnet."

"What is wrong with the one you have now?"

Harriett grinned, pulling at the ribbons under her chin to untie them. "Because this one is for you. The blue provides a needed contrast to your brown eyes and hair." She placed it on Grace's head, stepping back to admire her work.

"Why are you helping me? You cannot possibly wish me success in our wager."

Harriett laughed. "I do not think my assistance will make a difference. That man is never proposing marriage."

Grace tightened her jaw as her sister tied the ribbons of the bonnet securely under her chin.

She would see about that.

# Chapter 2

As the eldest son of the Earl of Coventry, Edward Beaumont had been given the courtesy title of Lord Ramsbury. But with his father afflicted with consumption, the public eagerly awaited the day he would become the new Lord Coventry.

Unless that day never came.

"You are disinheriting me?" Edward said in shock. His father's words struggled to sink into his mind. He had taken far too many glasses of brandy the night before, followed by far too many glasses of port. He hadn't meant to gamble away a tenth of the Coventry fortune in a game of cards.

He hadn't meant to do a lot of insensible things of late.

"For the third time, yes, Edward, I am disinheriting you." His father's stern voice sliced through his foggy mind. Edward's eyes adjusted to his surroundings, focusing on his father's gray hair and piercing blue eyes, reclined on his bed with a scowl.

Edward did not need to ask for clarification again. He fully understood the news his father had just delivered to him. His chest constricted with regret and anger, stirring up feelings of betrayal in his heart. He leaned forward on the chair beside his father's bed, his jaw clenching. "But the law requires that I assume the earldom upon your death. Surely you cannot surpass the laws of primogeniture without a great fight."

"I have been speaking with my solicitor, and we have worked through the legalities." His father drew a strenuous breath into his lungs. "Your disinheritance is very achievable in our family's situation, and has become even more desirable since your recent gamble. Henry will be assuming my title and the bulk of the fortune, not you."

Why had Edward thought it wise to place a wager on their fortune? If he hadn't gone to the deuced gaming hall in London he never would have found himself lacking the inheritance he had planned for his entire life. To see his younger brother Henry taking his place would be insufferable.

"Father, please forgive me for what I have done. I promise never to gamble again. Give me an opportunity to redeem my sin."

"It is not just this one folly that has made my decision," his father said in a harsh voice. "You have come to rely heavily on drink, and your behavior in society has been noted as disreputable. You are losing the favor of the public eye. You are disgracing the Beaumont name, as well as my title. You do not deserve it."

Despair crashed over Edward's shoulders, and he felt as if he were sinking into his chair. He had worked hard to preserve his public appearance amid the turmoil that he had been feeling for almost a year. He had met a woman, Miss Amelia Buxton, the previous summer. For the first time in his life he could imagine himself marrying, abandoning the life of a bachelor. The blasted woman had stolen his heart with the sole intent to gain information from him—information sought by the man she truly loved.

Edward had proposed to her, and she had rejected him. He was still feeling the effects of her rejection and deceit. He had kept the rejection hidden well from society, and had even tried to hide the effects of the rejection from himself, washing them away with brandy and sinful games. But it didn't work.

He had been sinking, slowly and steadily into a deep hole, and he didn't know how to escape. If his father disinherited him, the public would make even more assumptions about his character. They would question the charming persona he had perfected. His life would be even more disfigured than it already was.

"Give me a chance to redeem my *sins*." Edward begged his father with his eyes. "I will change. This inheritance is all I have."

"*Had*," his father corrected. "My decision has been made. Your mother is in agreement with my choice."

The feeling of betrayal dug deeper, twisting in Edward's stomach like a dull arrow. He would have suspected such betrayal from his father but never his mother. Lady Coventry doted on her children, but her gentleness had done little to tame her husband. His father had never cared for him, nor paid him a drop of attention. He only cared for himself, for his own designs and interests.

"Mother would never readily agree to such a drastic change," Edward said, unable to believe it.

His father grunted as he shifted his position under the blankets. "She did not agree readily," he sighed, "but the decision is not hers to make. It is her belief that you need only marry and your wife will somehow transform you into a genteel man. She wished for you to marry long ago. You could have, if only you had the decorum to settle for *one* woman."

"I did." Edward's eyes narrowed. "Last summer. And she declined my offer."

His father's eyebrows rose, becoming lost in the hair that splayed over his forehead. "Why did I not hear of this before?"

"I don't like speaking of it."

His father shrugged. "I'm not surprised. Your pride took a hit."

"My heart took a hit."

"Would you be willing to try again?"

Edward frowned. "She is married now."

His father shook his head, his eyes never leaving his son's face. "Not the same woman. Try to find a different woman you could marry."

Edward gave a hard laugh, cringing at the way it pounded through his aching skull. "I don't wish to marry a different woman. And what woman would want me without my inheritance?"

"You might keep your inheritance."

"What?" Edward wondered if his father's disease had reached his brain. "You just declared your decision to be final."

His father rubbed his chin, the sparse whiskers spreading between his fingers. "I will give you one more chance to keep your inheritance. But you will not like my stipulation." Edward guessed his father's words before he spoke them. "If you can manage to find a wife before I pass on, I will keep you as my heir. It will please your mother very much, and it is my greatest wish that she be happy after my death."

Edward eyed his father warily. The earl's dire condition had been progressing slowly over the last year, and in recent months had rendered him bedridden. He was only months from death, if not weeks. It wasn't that Edward lacked confidence—It wouldn't be difficult to find a woman willing to marry him. He had mothers and daughters lined up by the dozens in Brighton that wanted him—or rather—that wanted his fortune and the honor of his title. But he lacked the desire to marry. If he wished, he could find a woman willing to enter an engagement within a week and get the matter over with. The thought left him empty and numb inside. Did he have any other choice? If he refused he would be left with nothing.

"Fine. I will do it."

His father's eyes widened, as if surprised by his son's prompt reply.

"It will be simple," Edward said. "I'll be married before your death, I assure you. Engaged within a week."

His father puzzled over his words, a pained look in his expression. "There is no need to make such great haste with the endeavor. I will likely live longer than that."

"I will be efficient."

His father raised a scolding eyebrow. "But you must ensure you love the woman you choose." For such a stony man, his father's belief in true love was comical.

Edward stood, his arms tense at his sides. "I would rather keep my emotions uninvited. Much like the method you used in disinheriting me."

"Edward—"

"Good day, Father."

Turning on his heel, Edward moved to the door, exiting into the wide hallway of Clemsworth. His head pounded with a persistent headache, thwarting his balance as he moved toward the ballroom, where he knew his brother to be practicing his fencing. His mind spun as the realization of what he had just done crashed over him.

As he came closer to the ballroom, the usual sound of clashing metal reached his ears. He pushed open the double doors, slouching against the nearby wall until his brother noticed him.

Henry lowered his epee, lifting his mask onto his head, spilling his blond curls onto his forehead. "Edward." Henry's smile faltered. He muttered something to the friend with whom he had been practicing, Mr. Brooks. Without a moment of hesitation, Mr. Brooks exited the ballroom, throwing Edward a quick nod as he passed.

"When did you plan to tell me that father meant to disinherit me?" Edward pushed back from the wall as the ballroom doors swung shut behind Mr. Brooks. "You might have warned me."

Henry's eyes, the same sharp blue as his father's, rounded. "Father meant to disinherit you?"

Edward frowned with impatience. "Do not pretend you didn't know."

"I didn't, Edward. Upon my word." Henry rested his hand at his waist, his breathing still heavy from his fencing. "How did he manage to do it? The law is firm in the matter."

"Are you going to ask why he wished to disinherit me?"

Henry raised one eyebrow. "It's quite obvious. You did lose a tenth of the fortune in a game of cards. But surely he offered you a chance for redemption."

Edward studied his brother. The two were as opposite as any brothers could be. Henry clung to anything honorable, fulfilling every duty without question. If there were ever a decision to be made between right and wrong, he chose right, no matter the consequence to himself. His conscience had never been able to endure guilt, and his heart had never been able to choose hatred over love. In Edward's opinion, Henry loved too easily. Henry loved their father, despite his disinterest in his children for all their lives.

"He will only keep me as his heir if I find a wife before his death," Edward said, running his hand over his hair. He exhaled, long and slow. "It is not the ideal situation, but it will not be a problem. I shall find one before the end of the week."

Henry's jaw dropped. "That is very… efficient."

"Precisely."

"Don't you care to marry a woman you love?"

Edward gave an exasperated sigh. "You sound like Father."

Henry laughed, shrugging one shoulder as he moved to the weapon case on the wall, replacing his epee there. "I never thought you would be married before me. You do realize you will need to put a stop to your endless flirtations once you have a wife."

"My forthcoming flirtations this week will be enough to last my entire life." Edward managed a smile, the expression feeling strangely foreign.

Henry's laughter continued, shaking his broad shoulders. "Beware, women of Brighton, Lord Ramsbury is coming for one of you. Or all of you."

Edward laughed, sending pain shooting through his aching skull. "I haven't been to the assembly rooms for weeks." His laughter faded along with his smile. In the months following his rejection from Miss Buxton, he had continued making public appearances, trying to hide his dejection. But he had found the effort exhausting. The other women of Brighton would never make him feel the way she had made him feel. He was viewed as a prize, a reward to be earned by every visiting young lady in search of a husband. But Miss Buxton had treated him differently.

"It is time you changed that," Henry said. "The assembly rooms are the most social place in this town. I'm certain there are many pretty women gathered there as we speak."

Edward cracked his neck before squaring his shoulders. "Shall we get on with it then?"

"We?" Henry wiped the perspiration from his forehead as he lifted his mask from his head.

"You are accompanying me, are you not?"

"That is not a wise idea, brother. Every woman that glances your way will be distracted by my charm."

"Your fondest dream, perhaps."

Henry chuckled. "Very well. I'll come. But give me a moment to make myself presentable." He started toward the door but stopped, eyeing Edward with dismay. "I would also suggest that you shave before we leave."

Edward rubbed his bearded jaw, a wayward smile creeping over his mouth. "Only if you comb your hair."

"Are you certain? That would render you utterly inferior to me in appearance."

Edward smiled, leaning against the wall once again as Henry exited.

As Edward considered his new challenge, he decided he ought to determine a target. He could not simply charm every woman that crossed his path in the assembly rooms, or each individual lady would feel unimportant. He would choose just one today. He would test her, judge her reaction to his attention, estimate the extent of her devotion. All he needed to find was a pretty young woman with a respectable family. If she seemed promising, he would continue his pursuit. If not, he would choose a new lady the next day.

It would be simple. He would win back his inheritance before his father could have a chance to change his mind.

# Chapter 3

Taking the trip to the assembly rooms on foot had been a dreadful idea. Grace stopped on the cobblestone path, bending over to rub the back of her heel. "I had forgotten how long the walk was." She blew a puff of air upward to clear the hair that had fallen over her face. The weather was growing increasingly hot every day, manifested in the perspiration on her forehead.

Harriett smiled, breathing heavily from exertion as they climbed yet another hill. "Lord Ramsbury will find the flush of your cheeks endearing."

"You do not believe that," Grace said, turning her gaze toward the nearby ocean. The water was surprisingly calm today. Grace wished she felt calm. She didn't think she had ever felt so nervous in her entire life. But she was also determined, and enough determination could counter any fear.

Harriett laughed, lifting her skirts as she walked faster. "I believe he might find it endearing, but it will take more than a simple endearment to win a proposal from him."

Grace felt her hope fading with each step that took them closer to the assembly rooms. They passed through the town center, and Grace had to stop her sister from perusing the shops for the second time that day. The assembly rooms were close by. Grace's heart crashed against her ribs like the waves of the Brighton waters. She reminded herself that Lord Ramsbury was not even guaranteed to be there. It was entirely possible that he was still at his grand home, staring at himself in a looking glass, practicing his charming smile.

She gritted her teeth. How was she going to tolerate feeding the man's pride? It would be excruciating. And what if his proposal never came? He would carry on assuming he had stolen yet another heart he didn't intend to keep. She wouldn't be able to have her revenge.

When they passed through the hustle of the market, the path crossed through a thick patch of trees. Grace knew the assembly rooms rested just beyond them. She smoothed her hair, pulling two curls loose near the front of her face. Did she truly have the courage to do this? She could just surrender her pin money to Harriett now. The idea was becoming more and more attractive.

Lost in thought, she hadn't noticed the branch, stooping far beneath the rest as they passed under a tree. She gasped as the branch became interwoven with the lace on her bonnet. "Harriett!" she shrieked, lifting to her toes to minimize the pull of the branch.

Her sister turned, gasping in dismay. "My new bonnet! You've ruined it!" She rushed forward, rising on her toes to see the damage. Grace untied the ribbons from her chin, ducking out from under the tree. The bonnet still hung above her, swaying in the light breeze.

The sound of horse hooves reached her ears from behind, growing louder. Grace stepped out of the path, turning to face the approaching riders. She first saw the horses, one black and one chestnut brown. And then she saw the men riding them.

It was none other than Lord Ramsbury and his brother, Mr. Henry Beaumont.

Grace's breath caught. She whirled away from their sight, turning toward the tree that had captured her bonnet. Her heart pounded as the hooves slowed. She met Harriett's gaze, concealing her panic behind a pained smile. Harriett grinned, straightening her posture as her gaze slid past Grace and settled on the men behind her.

With a deep breath of fortitude, Grace turned around, slow and careful. Before she could meet Lord Ramsbury's eyes, she dropped her head in a deep bow, willing her legs not to shake. When she glanced up, she wished she hadn't.

Lord Ramsbury's eyes became fixed on hers, the blue striking even from a distance. He and his brother dismounted, and Grace took the opportunity to smooth her hair. Never in her walks to the assembly rooms had she ever encountered Lord Ramsbury. Why—*why* then did she have to encounter him today?

Gathering her bearings, she gave her most inviting smile as Lord Ramsbury examined her again. Did he recognize her? The last time they had spoken had been three years before. Grace had seen him at various balls and around the town since, but never in close proximity, and never in a situation where they were forced to make conversation. She didn't dare speak, for fear that he had forgotten that they had already been introduced.

He approached with slow steps, his saunter unmistakeable. The light that filtered through the trees reflected off the golden tones of his hair. Grace struggled to maintain his gaze, annoyance rising inside her as his smile grew. When he reached a distance of five feet from her, she assumed he would stop walking, but she was mistaken. He carried himself within two feet, dropping his head down to look directly into her eyes.

She swallowed when she smelled the fresh linen and soap mixed with an array of other pleasant masculine scents, wafting toward her from his skin and clothing. She scolded herself for enjoying it, tipping her head down bashfully. The men of the books she read enjoyed a woman with a coy demeanor. Grace peered at him from under her lashes, hoping to reflect an intrigued curiosity and shyness that he would find irresistible.

"Have we met?" he asked in a low voice. The sound spilled over her skin, tingling up her spine. Without realizing it, she took a step back, finding herself pressed against the tree that had stolen her bonnet. What was she doing? She was supposed to be flirting with him! She could not act as if she wanted to escape him. That is not at all what a heroine would do when encountered with a handsome gentleman. Or rather—a handsome scoundrel.

"I'm not certain I recall making your acquaintance," she said with a demure smile, maintaining his piercing gaze with effort. "Therefore we should not be speaking."

"Yes, but it is permitted when the situation demands it." He nodded at the bonnet hanging from the tree. "When a beautiful lady is in distress, for example."

She contained her disapproval, offering a giggle instead. "I assume you must be Lord Ramsbury. You are quite well-known throughout Brighton." *Well known for disregarding social rules.*

He studied her, his eyes flashing with a hint of recognition before clearing again. His smile widened. "I don't recall meeting you. If I had, I'm certain I would not have forgotten such a beautiful face."

She bit the inside of her cheek to stop herself from offering the retort that burned on her tongue. She gave a coy laugh, twirling one strand of her hair around her finger. "Oh, your flattery is too much, my lord. A short time from now I'm certain you will have forgotten me."

He shook his head, stepping even closer. She pressed instinctively into the trunk of the tree, unable to escape. "A short time from now I hope to be much further acquainted with you."

Her heart jumped in her chest. She couldn't believe her good fortune. She had done little to encourage Lord Ramsbury's attention, and he had already expressed an interest in furthering their acquaintance.

He touched a hand to his heart. "Please, do put my curiosity to rest and tell me your name."

"Miss Grace Weston." Eager to divert his intense attention, she turned toward Harriett, who had been watching the ordeal with obvious surprise. "And this is my elder sister, Miss Harriett Weston."

Lord Ramsbury's gaze flicked to Harriett, and he offered a quick bow and smile before returning his attention fully to Grace. She stared up at him. It was more difficult than she had imagined it would be to perform her act. Every instinct told her to snub him, to show him how uninterested she truly was in him. To insult him until the glowing arrogance left his brooding eyes. She felt as if she were sixteen again, trapped in a ballroom corner while

Lord Ramsbury led her to believe things that weren't true, taking her heart in his fist. He had toyed with her emotions, never investing his own.

But this time there was a drastic difference. She too had left her heart and emotions tucked safely away at Weston Manor. All was fair in this battle.

"Are you on a visit to Brighton? It is becoming quite famous, after all." Lord Ramsbury's sickeningly flirtatious voice cut through Grace's thoughts.

"We have grown up here in Brighton," Grace said, proud of herself for keeping the annoyance out of her voice. "We live on the east side of the shops."

"I see." He flashed her a smile that was meant to be charming. "I do recognize the name Weston. It is a pity I have not yet been acquainted with your family."

"It is no matter. We are beneath your notice, my lord."

She bit her lip in regret. She had just implied that she thought him to be condescending.

He didn't seem to catch her implications, a low chuckle escaping him. "And where are you traveling now?" He gestured at the path on which they had been walking.

"The assembly rooms." Grace searched for a plausible excuse for their excursion there. "We thought we might engage some new company in a game of whist."

Lord Ramsbury tipped his head even closer close enough for Grace to see the line of navy blue that outlined the bright blue of his irises. "How fortuitous that whist is a game that requires four players. My brother and I would be honored to join you and your sister."

Grace thought she heard a quiet gasp of dismay from Harriett but she couldn't be certain. Grace's heart thudded. Could Lord Ramsbury be genuinely interested in her? Could she have a real chance to win her bargain with

Harriett? She stopped herself. This had happened once before. He could very well be merely giving himself a bit of entertainment.

She changed her mind about acting simpering and coy. The last time, at her first ball, she had been too shy, and he had forgotten her. It was imperative that she make herself *unforgettable* this time.

"The honor would be ours to join you, my lord," she said, forcing herself to lean toward him as she spoke.

He grinned triumphantly, throwing his brother a glance.

Mr. Beaumont, who had been standing near his horse in silence, stepped forward. "It is a pleasure to meet you, Miss Weston, Miss Grace. But I must warn you. The Beaumont men are unrivaled in cards." He gave a half smile, eyeing his brother.

Grace gave her most flirtatious laugh, the sound much higher-pitched than she had intended. She cleared her throat, a smile pasted on her face. "When it comes to cards, it is the Weston women that are quite dangerous."

Lord Ramsbury's gaze roamed over her, maintaining his wicked grin. "I can think of other ways in which you are dangerous."

Grace's cheeks burned at the insinuation. Annoyance almost cut through her act, but she maintained her coquettish demeanor. "You are a wicked man," she teased. If only she could tell him how wicked he truly was.

He laughed before taking two steps forward, untangling her bonnet from where it hung above her. "How did you lose your bonnet to this branch?" he asked, approaching her with the headpiece. He placed it on top of her curls, his movements slow as he loosened the ribbons, bringing them underneath her chin. His hands brushed her neck and jaw as he tied them, sending uncalled for shivers across her shoulders. His familiarity shocked her, causing a blush to burn across her cheeks. The man had no respect for the rules of society. No respect at all.

"I did not see the branch above me," she replied. "It whisked the bonnet right off my head. How fortunate I am to have had you come to my rescue." She pressed her lips together, looking into his enraging eyes.

Oh, how she hated to flatter him.

"As I said before, I am always glad to help such a beautiful woman in distress." He winked, gesturing to his horse with a flourish. "May I offer you my horse for the remainder of the ride to the assembly? You will need to be well rested if you hope to conquer me in whist."

Grace giggled, appalled at herself for even being capable of making the sound. How did he find her alluring? She viewed her behavior as quite the opposite. She would never act so unintelligently. "You are very kind, my lord."

Stopping beside the black horse, Lord Ramsbury made a step with his hands, helping to hoist her onto the saddle. He clutched the reins in his own hand from where he stood on the ground. Mr. Beaumont led Harriett to his horse as well, and Grace caught her gaze as she passed. Harriett had never been one to easily conceal her emotions, so Grace could clearly discern the shock in her sister's eyes. Grace was every bit as surprised as her sister.

The two men guided the horses through the trees, careful to avoid any stooping branches. Grace's mind spun as they made their way to the assembly rooms. Lord Ramsbury's flirting had become even more incorrigible than it had been before. She hadn't thought it possible. How could she ensure his attention didn't end after today?

"Are you a skilled rider?" she asked, straightening her posture as she looked down at him from atop the horse.

He laughed, as if the answer were painfully obvious. "Of course."

"I suspected as much. One in your physical condition could only be regarded as a skilled rider. And your wealth would allow you to stable many fine horses with which to practice."

Lord Ramsbury chuckled, a deep, sultry sound. "You are quite right, Miss Grace. And one with your lovely physical appearance could only look so pristine atop a horse."

With a forced giggle, Grace twirled a lock of her hair, pretending not to be sickened by his flattery. Why had she agreed to this? It was already exhausting and it had only just begun. "Please, my lord, you flatter me too much."

"It would be impossible not to flatter you. I have never met a woman in possession of such beauty."

Grace wondered how many times he had uttered those words. Unable to help it, she shared a secret glance of irritation with Harriett. Harriett covered her mouth with one gloved hand, concealing her smile.

"And I have never met a man in possession of such *audacity*." She said the word with a smile, as if it tasted like a freshly baked cake, not the hidden insult that it was.

His deep chuckle reached her ears from below. He tipped his head to the side, squinting against the sun to look at her, curiosity burning in his eyes.

Grace felt she might vomit.

When they reached the assembly rooms, Lord Ramsbury tied his black horse before offering his hand to let Grace down. As she slid from the saddle, she let go of his hand too quickly, stumbling into him as she reached the ground. His hands caught her by the waist, lingering there as he stared into her eyes.

She jumped back without thinking, quickly covering her misstep with a quiet laugh. "I have never been a very skilled rider myself."

"Yet you are very skilled at finding a reason to fall into my arms."

"I did not! I mean—" Grace cut off her own words with a laugh, hoping to cover her mistake. She lowered her eyes. "Your arms are so very inviting."

Harriett squeaked, her dismayed gasp nearly escaping yet again. Grace warned her with a look, her cheeks burning as Lord Ramsbury gave another of his infuriating chuckles, leading the small party into the ballroom area of the assembly.

Grace noticed several eyes darting to Lord Ramsbury, followed by a smattering of whispers behind gloved hands and fans. The card room rested on the left side, and held very few inhabitants. An elderly couple sat at the far card table, engaged in a game of piquet, while a group of gentlemen played near the adjacent wall. Lord Ramsbury chose a table nearest the door, offering Grace the first chair.

"What shall the teams be?" he asked as Harriett and Mr. Beaumont took their seats.

"Ladies against gentlemen, of course," Harriett said.

"Yes," Grace agreed. "How else will we prove our superiority at whist?"

"You will not prove anything," Lord Ramsbury said, taking his seat beside Grace and across from his brother. "Because you will lose."

"I accept your challenge." Grace smiled. To beat Lord Ramsbury in a game of whist would bring enough satisfaction to hold her over until he proposed and she could reject him. *If he proposed.*

He turned his head to look at her. "If we win, you must allow me to call upon you tomorrow morning."

Shocked by his request, Grace forgot her charade for a moment, her eyes rounding. "Tomorrow morning?"

"Indeed."

"And if you lose?"

Half his mouth lifted in a smile. "Then I shall wait most impatiently until the afternoon."

Grace wondered if her ears had deceived her. Lord Ramsbury had shared a ballroom with her on many occasions, but he had never paid her any notice since her first ball. Why now?

She glanced at him from beneath a sheet of fluttering lashes. "It seems we have a bargain."

"But we shall not call it that," he said. "You know it is not proper for a lady to make a bargain."

Grace exchanged a glance with Harriett before returning her attention to Lord Ramsbury. "A proper lady does not condone outrageous flirting either, yet you have convinced me to allow both."

He placed one elbow on the card table, leaning closer to her. "I *am* known to be quite persuasive."

"Shall we begin the game?" Mr. Beaumont said in a quick voice, casting his brother a look of exasperation. Lord Ramsbury straightened his posture, taking the deck of cards in his hands. Amusement welled up inside Grace. It was as if she and Lord Ramsbury were attempting to outdo the other in flirtation. Little did he know that she was only pretending to enjoy his company. The fact that he wished to see her the next day filled her with hope and dread at once. She had a fair chance at winning her wager with Harriett, but it meant she would have to spend more time controlling her urge to drag her fingernails across Lord Ramsbury's perfect face.

"Would you like to deal the cards?" He extended the deck to Grace and she took it, making sure to brush her fingers over his. The touch brought far too much sensation to her own skin, leading her to pull the deck away fast, snatching it from his hand.

She dealt the cards around the table, ignoring the heat on her cheeks. "For trump..." she flipped the last card of the deck, placing it in the center of the table. "Hearts."

"My favorite," Lord Ramsbury said, fanning out his cards as he studied them. Grace glanced across the table at Harriett, hoping to get a hint of the quality of her hand. Grace studied her own cards, keeping them close to her so Lord Ramsbury couldn't sneak a glance.

As the game progressed, the Beaumonts managed to lead by four points. Grace continued her flirting and teasing banter with Lord Ramsbury, who returned it readily. She was impressed with his wit, but nothing more. He was every bit as pompous as she remembered, fully aware of his affecting smiles and gazes, and the way his whispered voice beside her ear sent her heart into a frenzy. How, after all the hatred she had built against the man, did he manage to affect her? Could she still inhabit feelings of attraction toward him? She demanded that it was impossible, closing her heart and mind to the possibility.

By the fifth round, Grace and Harriett scored five points, winning the game. Grace turned to Lord Ramsbury, unable to help herself from flaunting her victory.

He sat back in his chair, a pompous smirk on his face. "We intentionally allowed you to win."

Grace scoffed. "You did not. Even with your sincere effort, our victory was easily won, was it not, Harriett?"

Her sister stared at her with wide eyes, as if unwilling to contribute to the verbal sparring with Lord Ramsbury.

"Well, I have won either way." Lord Ramsbury reclined in his chair. "For I will have the privilege of seeing you, Miss Grace, again tomorrow." He winked. "Even if I must now wait until the afternoon. I shall call upon you then."

Grace brought a simpering smile back to her face. "I look forward to it most eagerly."

After flashing her another grin, Lord Ramsbury and his brother stood, leading the ladies back outside. Grace politely declined the offer to ride their horses back to Weston Manor, claiming that she enjoyed the exercise of walking.

She had never been more deceitful in her life than she had today.

When the men rode away, leaving Grace and Harriett by the doors of the assembly rooms, Grace turned to her sister. "Well, that was certainly unexpected."

Harriett giggled before her smile quickly turned to a frown. "But you will not win."

"And why not? He seemed quite interested in furthering our acquaintance."

"Yes, but is that not how he behaved last time? I suspect he will not even call upon you tomorrow as he promised."

Grace bit her lip. Could her sister be right?

"He enjoys flirting, as you know," Harriett said. "And you proved yourself to be just as much of an outrageous flirt as he. You are providing him with a bit of fun. Soon he will grow tired of you and move along to the next woman that can tolerate his company."

"It is possible." Grace puzzled over Harriett's words. "But it is also possible that he will not grow tired of me this time." How could she make certain his feelings for her grew enough to elicit a proposal of marriage? Men like Lord Ramsbury did not settle for one lady. Now that she had his attention, she would need to be perfectly charming, polite, and accepting of his flattery. She would need to be entertaining and humorous and subtly romantic. She had flattered him too much now to lose her chance to reject him. There would be no turning back.

Part of her burned with guilt, but she pushed it away. He had treated her like a game once, so now she would do the same. An eye for a stunning blue eye, a tooth for a sparkling white tooth.

Or something of the sort.

"You were correct about one thing, Harriett," Grace said as they began their walk. "Flattering him *is* torturous."

Harriett tossed her head back with a laugh. "But your act was so convincing! I'm certain you have him fooled."

"Was it truly?" Grace had felt like a complete ninny trying to be so coquettish.

Harriett nodded, bursting into laughter. "Mama and Papa would be appalled if they had seen it."

Grace covered her mouth, suddenly embarrassed as she thought of all the things she had said to Lord Ramsbury. "He enjoyed my words so very much, didn't he? I might be ill." She pretended to gag, intensifying her sister's laughter.

"You must admit he is handsome."

"He is," Grace volunteered. "There is no question. But he knows it, and he flaunts it, which makes him much less attractive. Good heavens, he is so infuriating! He thinks he can win any woman in the world with a few charming words. It will be beneficial to his pride to be rejected by me."

Harriett raised a scolding finger. "He has not made any offer yet."

"That is true." Grace chewed the nail of her index finger as they walked. "But Harriett, even if I do lose, will you please consider Mr. Harrison?"

"Grace!"

She smiled, keeping her mouth closed as they finished the long walk home.

# Chapter 4

"Well done, brother," Henry said, slapping Edward on the back as they dismounted at Clemsworth. "I will never question your ability again."

Edward had spent the ride in deep thought, considering his next plan of action. The moment he had seen Miss Grace he had chosen her. Mostly because she was closer in proximity to him than the other Weston daughter, who was also quite beautiful. But he had always had a preference for brown eyes. And Miss Grace certainly possessed a stunning pair of eyes.

Something about her had seemed familiar. He was fairly certain they had met once before, but he couldn't place the time. She had readily accepted his compliments and offered an array of her own, something he had never experienced from a woman. He found it fascinating, if not slightly frustrating.

He had once been drawn to Miss Buxton because of her resistance to his flattery. He had enjoyed the challenge, and had ultimately lost. Perhaps a woman like Miss Grace was just what he needed. No challenge at all to win her favor. Since he had been rejected by Miss Buxton, he no longer felt inclined to undertake a challenge.

"To consider that I could have been father's heir," Henry said, shaking his head. He gave a teasing smile. "But I'd rather have you keep what is rightfully yours."

Edward gave a small smile—his time with Miss Grace had exhausted his storage of wide ones. "Are you really so certain she will have me?"

"Her attention toward you strongly suggested that she would." Henry chuckled. "Every woman desires to be married to a future earl."

Edward's skin prickled. "If I weren't to receive a title... do you suppose she would still favor me?"

"That is doubtful. Why do you suppose I am still unattached?"

Edward laughed, but didn't feel it. He shouldn't have hated his title so much. He was going to marry to keep it, after all. But he often wondered what it would be like if he didn't have one. He wouldn't feel the persistent need to maintain his public image. He wouldn't have to wonder if every woman he met cared for him or only for his possessions.

They walked through the front doors of Clemsworth, stopping in the entry hall. "Where do you plan to take her tomorrow?" Henry asked.

Edward rubbed his jaw, still unaccustomed to the smoothness of it. "I will take her to see the royal pavilion and continue to convince her that she cannot live without me."

Henry bent over in laughter as he walked toward the opposite hall. "I wish you good fortune in that endeavor."

"I do not need it." Edward grinned as his brother left the entry. The vast space filled with silence, and Edward drew a heavy breath. His act would need to be very convincing the next day. He could not grow lazy now. If he succeeded he would give Miss Grace what she was after, and secure the same for himself: his wealth and title.

With emptiness in his chest, he walked toward his chambers.

---

As he had hoped, the next day brought warm weather—warm enough for a day out of doors with Miss Grace. When Edward had told his father about his plans to court her, he had been surprised that Edward had found a lady so quickly. Once he had recovered from his shock and masked censure, he had grudgingly helped Edward with the arrangements.

Edward had requested that the servants prepare a grand meal for him to take in a picnic basket. By one of the clock, he departed from Clemsworth. His father was familiar with the Weston family, claiming that they had been in attendance at more than one of the balls they had hosted at Clemsworth. Edward had met so many people at those balls—so many pretty young ladies in particular—that he hadn't recognized the Weston daughters. He couldn't believe he had forgotten Miss Grace and her dark brown eyes, bronze hair, pleasing figure, and unblemished skin. Her smile was notable as well.

When he arrived at her home, she met him in the drawing room. She wore a pale pink gown that draped over her curves becomingly, with two dark curls framing her face beneath her straw bonnet. Her expression lifted when she saw him, her cheeks coloring slightly as she studied his appearance.

"Miss Grace, you look quite lovely this afternoon." He extended his arm which she took with enthusiasm. He guided her toward the front door, staring down at the brim of her bonnet, waiting for his next glimpse at her teasing brown eyes.

She tipped her head up, granting his wish. "The public would only expect to see beauty on the arm of Lord Ramsbury." She cast him a smile, only half looking at him. Her hand was stiff around his elbow.

"And they shall." He touched the curl that hung around her face, brushing it aside. His movement only caused her hand to become more tense. Was she nervous to be in his company? How endearing. A sly smile pulled on his lips.

She gave a quiet laugh as they stepped into the morning sun. "We must wait for my aunt." She glanced back at the house expectantly. He followed her gaze to where a rather large woman descended the steps, a scowl on her reddened face.

Miss Grace's defined eyebrows tightening in look of concern. "She does not enjoy chaperoning."

He stole another look at her aunt as she trudged over the grass behind them. The image struck him as humorous, but he couldn't decipher if Miss Grace thought the same.

"Aunt Christine, please meet Lord Ramsbury."

The nettled woman greeted him with a huff, nodding for the sake of propriety. He straightened his posture, returning his gaze to the ground ahead. He barely caught the look of amusement in Miss Grace's expression before it turned thoughtful. "Where are we going?"

"To the royal pavilion. I thought you might enjoy a picnic in the public gardens nearby. The pavilion grounds are exquisite to look upon in the spring."

"How diverting," she said. "I never grow tired of looking upon the pavilion. I can only dream of living in such grandeur. The Prince Regent is a very blessed man."

Edward's brow twinged with annoyance. Henry was correct about Miss Grace. She aspired to great wealth, and Edward was her way of achieving it. He told himself not to care, but it frustrated him nonetheless. He cleared his expression before she could wonder if something was amiss.

Edward offered to assist their chaperone onto the back seat of the barouche, but she refused, climbing up with great effort. He helped Miss Grace into the contraption before stepping in beside her, taking the reins in his hands. He turned toward her, moving the slightest bit closer, to the point where his leg rested against hers. "Tell me more concerning yourself, Miss Grace," he said, flicking the reins and setting the horses in motion.

Her eyes lifted to his, her head tipping to the side. "What do you wish to know?"

"Well, you have already proven yourself to be in possession of a very intelligent mind through your strategy in cards. What other talents do you possess?"

"You are inviting me to boast?" She gave him another of her flirtatious smiles.

"A lady's accomplishments are something to be readily declared to men, are they not? Tell me."

She laughed, deep thought evident in her eyes. "I love to rea—" Her mouth closed as if she were reconsidering her words. "Rehearse the pianoforte," she said finally. "And I am a skilled harpist as well. And I am an artist. I stitch, crochet, and am fluent in French." Her voice came out quick.

He raised his eyebrows. "That is an extensive list. I am impressed."

She shrugged one shoulder. "I prefer not to waste time on unproductive activities."

"Such as?"

She licked her lips, her gaze darting back and forth in thought. "Reading fictional stories."

"I enjoy reading fictional stories," he said.

Her eyes flew to his, wide with shock. "Truly?"

"No." He chuckled. He gazed down at her, surprised to see a look of disappointment in her expression.

"I was only jesting. Did you believe me?"

Her brow furrowed before becoming smooth again. She offered him a pleasant smile. "Yes. Your wit is unmatched, my lord."

He nudged her leg with his knee, pressing closer to her until their arms touched. She drew a quick breath, her gaze fixed straight ahead. He smiled. The tactic had never failed to gain a reaction. "I beg to differ. I believe my wit is well-matched by your own." As they passed a small meadow, he shifted the reins to one hand, taking her hand from her lap, wrapping it up in his.

Her gaze lifted slowly upward as she drew an audible breath. Her eyes flicked to their hands before coming to rest on his face. An endearing blush crossed over her cheeks. "But not if you continue to do things that steal my wits from me."

He entwined his fingers in hers, tipping his face closer. "You have uncovered my nefarious plan."

She blinked, an inquisitive intelligence burning in her eyes before becoming replaced with a coyness that did not seem to fit. He slipped his hand away from hers to better control the horses, leading them toward the approaching gardens.

"We have arrived." Edward stepped down from the barouche after bringing the horses to a halt. They were stopped in front of the garden park neighboring the royal pavilion. He turned to offer his hand to Miss Grace, presenting her with his most alluring smile. She took his hand, threading her fingers around his arm once her feet touched the ground.

The royal pavilion loomed nearby. The interior, Edward had heard, held the most grand furnishings in the county, and the exterior was modeled after the architecture of China and India, with large spires and ridged domes built in pale stone. The building donned countless windows, and the surrounding land had been groomed to perfection, with colorful blossoms adorning the trees.

He led Miss Grace to the public gardens overlooking the pavilion, motioning for her to sit on a wooden bench surrounded by flowered bushes. She fit in quite nicely among the blossoms, their beauty unmatched by her own. Taking a seat beside her, he carefully deposited the picnic basket on the grass. Miss Grace's aunt glanced lazily at her niece before finding her own place beneath a tree several feet away, withdrawing a ball of yarn and needles from her bag.

He was pleased Miss Grace did not have an overbearing chaperone. It would make romancing her much easier.

Edward uncovered the basket, tossing Miss Grace a smile over his shoulder. "I hope you are hungry."

Her pretty eyes rounded at the sight of the interior of the basket. Suspecting that she only desired his wealth, he had prepared the feast to showcase the grandeur she would be indulging in for the rest of her life if she married him. He didn't mean to draw out their courtship longer than necessary, so he needed to employ every tactic at his disposal.

"I hope you like compote of pears and nougat almond cake." He had noticed her eyes jump quickly to the desserts.

"Pears are my favorite fruit," she said. "How did you know?"

He grinned inwardly, pleased with his own intuition. "It was an accurate presumption."

Her smile grew. "I find it fascinating how well you understand me when we have only recently met."

"I wish I understood much more. Tell me about your family." Edward leaned over, preparing a plate of an assortment of food for her as he listened.

"Harriett is the eldest child, and I am the second. Our parents had no sons. Just Harriett and me, and our kitten, Lilac." She gestured at their chaperone. "My aunt and her husband live nearby, as well as another uncle of mine, one whose wife is no longer living. He is practically like a father to me. He quite enjoys treating his nieces like queens."

Edward glanced up at her as he withdrew her plate from the basket. The way she spoke of her uncle reminded him of his own uncle, one who had passed away in recent years.

He studied her, noting that her smile seemed different, a more genuine nature to it as she spoke. The moment her gaze met his, her smile stiffened, turning decidedly more coy. She bit her lip as she looked at the plate. "How do you expect me to eat all of that, my lord?"

"You did say you loved pears."

She laughed, a choppy, shrill sound. He wondered if

he could bear listening to such a laugh for his entire life. It sounded false and manipulated.

"I do love them," she said. "But I do not need twenty."

"There are not *twenty*." He counted the slices of pear on her plate. "Only thirteen."

She laughed, a gentler sound than before. "I have never been very skilled at mathematics."

"I enjoy mathematics," Edward said.

Her brow raised in doubt. "*You* enjoy mathematics?"

Why had he admitted that he enjoyed such an intellectual thing? Society would not expect that he cared for anything but sociality and games. Apparently that was Miss Grace's presumption of him. He wanted to ask her why it was so surprising, but thought better of it.

"I do." He searched for a change of subject. He needed to set to work romancing her before she could regain her wits. "Do you enjoy dancing?"

"Dancing?" she looked at him with confusion, likely at the abrupt change of topic. "Yes, of course."

He set down his plate, moving to stand in front of her. "I know this is not a ballroom…" he flashed a smile, "but would you honor me with a dance?"

Her surprise called out in every line of her face. She glanced at her aunt, who had turned herself away, her eyes fixed on the distant ocean. "There is no music."

"You are wrong. There is music if you listen to the sea." He extended his hand to her, fixing his gaze on hers. She placed her hand in his and he pulled her up. Giving her one final tug, he wrapped his other arm around her waist, bringing her close.

Her breath caught as her eyes flew to his. Her expression faltered in dismay before she replaced her smile, her eyelashes fluttering in obvious flirtation. Why did women always feel the need to blink so rapidly? He found it strangely irritating.

Raising their entwined hands to the side, he waited as she reluctantly rested her hand on his shoulder.

"A waltz?" Her throat bobbed with a nervous swallow.

He smiled, tipping his head down closer to hers as he took the first step in the square. Her feet followed, hesitant and slow. They turned to the sound of the distant waves as they splashed against the shore.

She gave a soft laugh, glancing down at their feet before returning her gaze to his. "I have never danced outside of a ballroom."

"Nor have I," he said, willing his eyes to convey sincerity. He needed Miss Grace to believe she was special, the sole recipient of his affections. As she stared up at him in obvious adoration, he wondered how much longer he would even need to continue with his act. She would likely accept his proposal if he offered it that very moment. He smiled inwardly. He was even more skilled than he thought.

"You are a talented dancer," she said. "Even without music."

"There *is* music," he said. "The sea. Don't you hear it?"

She turned her attention toward the nearby ocean, closing her eyes. He noted the dark sweep of her lashes and brows and smoothness of her complexion—the natural pinkness to her cheeks. He had chosen one of the most beautiful women of Brighton, he was certain. Even if her laugh was vexing and her motives for marrying him frustrating, at least he would not tire of looking upon her.

Miss Grace's eyes popped opened. Her irises were such a dark brown that they were nearly indistinguishable from her pupils. But he was close enough to see the difference, and to see them shrink with the sudden increase of light. "I heard it," she whispered, smiling.

He pressed his hand into the small of her back, bringing her even closer. "If music be the food of love, play on."

Her face contorted in shock. "Shakespeare?"

"Twelfth Night, Orsino."

She corrected her features, but he caught the sheen of surprise that crossed her face. "I thought you did not enjoy fictional stories," she muttered.

"I did have a relentless tutor that forced me to read in my youth." He chuckled, expecting her to laugh at his comment. But she remained silent, a crease appearing between her eyebrows. What had he done? "Is there something amiss?"

She tipped her face up to his, a fresh smile on her lips. "Nothing at all."

Miss Grace puzzled him. Her countenance seemed to change more than the average woman. One moment she was outrightly flirtatious and the next she was rather serious. Even as he studied her face, her smile appeared somewhat forced. Even so, the dimple that it caused to appear on the left side of her chin was lovely to say the least.

"You ought not to smile at me so often," he said. "You might tempt me to do something dishonorable." If he had the audacity to kiss her now then she would marry him for certain. He considered the idea, but thought it nearly impossible to steal a kiss quickly enough to evade the eyes of her chaperone. When he did kiss her, he couldn't afford for it to be *quick*. He needed to convince her to marry him, and a quick kiss would not showcase his talent at all.

She giggled as he released her waist, guiding her into

a spin before bringing her back into his arms. He was pleased she had chosen a lenient chaperone. Her aunt scarcely even watched them, busy knitting away from a distance. If they were seen dancing so closely, his hand at her waist, her reputation would be compromised. But he had chosen an empty area of the gardens to entertain her, where no sneaking gossip could catch sight of them.

"Dishonorable? You do not strike me as a dishonorable man," she said as their waltz brought them closer to a nearby rose bush.

"Perhaps you do not know me well enough."

"I daresay you have never misused a woman and her emotions without the intention to marry her. I suspect you have never made promises of your affection and forgotten them. You seem to be a gentleman of an honorable sort." She stared into his eyes, her own wide with innocence.

Edward's jaw tightened. He wished she were right, but he knew his character to be quite the opposite. Before Miss Buxton had broken his heart, he had not realized how fragile a heart truly was. He had been careless with a number of young women, claiming their affection and more than his share of hearts, always viewing his pursuits as a game. Until he knew how it felt, he had been oblivious to the pain he had caused.

"Your estimation of my character is not entirely accurate," he said before he could stop the words.

She blinked. "How so?"

"Well, I—" He stumbled for a response. "I am a gentleman of the *most* honorable sort."

Her high-pitched laugh in close proximity to his ear came off even more unpleasant than before. "You are a terrible tease, my lord."

He stopped their dance, giving her his most pleasant smile, forced as it was. "Does that make me less honorable?"

"No. It simply makes you more charming." She drew out her words, her own voice low and alluring. Her eyes, sparking with intelligence, did not match the simpering behavior she was performing. He brushed aside his concerns. Miss Grace seemed to be smitten with him, determined to marry him and to claim his fortune. There was no point in prolonging their courtship.

They spent the next hour finishing their meal, talking of insignificant things, and Edward carried on with his act, eager for the day when their engagement was secure and he would no longer have to pretend her laugh did not vex him.

When they married, she wouldn't genuinely love him, and he wouldn't particularly care for her. They would marry for the purpose of his retained inheritance and her attained fortune. The sooner he could relieve himself of the pressure of his father's requirement the better. As he considered her complete infatuation with him, he decided that a proposal the next day would without a doubt be happily received and accepted by Miss Grace.

As he returned her to her house, he stopped near the front door of her family's modest home. After expressing his intention to see her the next day, he placed a passionate kiss on the back of her hand in farewell. Her cheeks flushed and she smiled as he took his leave. He waved from his seat atop his barouche as he steered his horses down the road.

The moment Edward was out of her line of sight, he slumped against the back of his seat, slackening his grip on the reins. Miss Grace was beautiful, and while he was proud of himself for securing her affection so quickly, it was bothersome how little effort it had required. It was as if she had no mind and will of her own, her smiles and laughter so easily given. In truth, he had expected more of a challenge.

But was this not what he wanted? To secure a simple-minded, pretty wife that would appease his parents and society's demand? Yes. His brow furrowed as he tried to rid his mind of her harsh laugh. The moment they were engaged he would make it his goal to never make her laugh. He couldn't possibly live with such a blasted sound in his ear every day.

Releasing a slow breath, he closed his eyes, a strong ache throbbing once again on his skull.

# Chapter 5

The moment Grace stepped through the door, she turned away from her aunt, barely controlling her urge to scoff in a manner that would challenge even Harriett's display. Lord Ramsbury was infuriating! She wiped the back of her hand where he had kissed her against her skirts, willing the rate of her heart to slow. He was infuriating in many ways, but the most prevalent reason being that he still managed to affect her, even with his obtuse efforts to woo her.

He was more skilled than she remembered.

"Thank you for chaperoning me, Aunt Christine," Grace said, forcing a smile of gratitude to her cheeks.

Aunt Christine, the prim woman that she was, withdrew her fan, batting it at her neck as she spoke. "He does seem quite attached to you. A proposal is in order if he continues with his attention. You must tread carefully. If he were to stop his pursuit of you now your reputation will suffer. And I don't suspect a man like Lord Ramsbury would bat an eye at tarnishing your reputation."

Grace had left out the detail that she did not intend to ever marry him. She had withheld that detail from everyone who knew of her excursion with Lord Ramsbury that day, including her parents. Her mother and father had been shocked to hear of her new courtship, already knowing of her distaste for Lord Ramsbury. She had managed to convince them that he seemed to be an improved man, though she didn't believe it. They had then expressed their exuberant approval of the match.

She would hate to disappoint them.

"Do you think he will propose?" Grace asked Aunt Christine as they walked toward the drawing room.

"It appears that way." Her aunt snapped her fan shut in surprise at the sight of her brother, Grace's widowed uncle, standing near the pianoforte.

"Uncle Cornelius!" Grace smiled. "I did not expect to see you here."

He stepped forward with a grin. "I heard a rumor about a certain courtship, and I could not bear the thought of remaining at home without discovering all the details."

Uncle Cornelius was the respectable Baron of Hove, the eldest brother of Grace's mother and Aunt Christine. Since his wife had passed away five years previous, he spent most of his days devoted to his family to fill the void of loneliness in his life. His marriage had brought no children, so he treated Grace and Harriett as his own daughters. He was the most eccentric member of their family, and Grace would not have it any other way.

His yellow waistcoat stretched across his rounded belly. As he smoothed the wrinkles from it, he slipped his hand into his jacked with a gasp. "Oh! What could this be?" His blue eyes sparkled with mirth, his eyebrows raising nearly high enough to surpass his receding hairline. Withdrawing his hand, he pulled out a small box, complete with a pink ribbon.

Grace laughed. "What is it?"

"A gift for you, my dear." He smiled, extending the box to her. "A lady's first courtship is to be celebrated, especially when it involves a future earl." He winked.

"You are too generous!" Grace took the box, guilt twisting in her stomach. How dejected her family would be when she refused Lord Ramsbury's proposal. If one came, of course. Grace still suspected he was toying with her.

She threw her uncle a look of gratitude as she untied the ribbon, lifting the lid from the box. Resting inside on a pillow of silk was a delicate necklace. The slim chain donned a small green pendant, sparkling in the well-lit room.

"It is lovely, thank you, Uncle. I will treasure it always."

His smile stretched wide. "Do not tell Harriett. I suspect she will be envious. When she begins her first courtship I will have the town jeweler design one to match."

Grace closed the box, looking up with a grin. "Not to worry, I have no doubt she will begin courting very soon." Excitement surged in her chest at the thought of Harriett and Mr. Harrison together. The romantic within her sighed with contentment. If Grace won the wager it would all be worth it to see Harriett courting William.

Uncle Cornelius's eyes grew wide, the blue almost as piercing as Lord Ramsbury's. As Grace thought of Lord Ramsbury's eyes, her heart gave a wayward leap. Why must he be so handsome? Everything would be much easier if he resembled a toad.

"Who is the man that has captured Harriett's attention?" Uncle Cornelius prodded. "Please tell me so I may determine if he wins my approval or not."

"Do you approve of Lord Ramsbury?" Grace asked, puzzled. Uncle Cornelius was fully aware of Lord Ramsbury's somewhat unscrupulous ways.

Her uncle tapped his chin, deep wrinkles creasing the sides of his eyes as he smiled. "I have only met him briefly, so most of what I know of him comes from the gossip of society. Often that is very different from the truth. Surely you know him better than I. And you are a very intelligent young lady; I trust you would not let an attachment develop with a man that is not worthy of you. Perhaps I will invite him to dinner at my home," he mused. "Then I may decipher his character more fully."

Grace had just spent hours with Lord Ramsbury away from the public, and he had still been superficial and pompous. Was he even capable of deep and meaningful thought? He seemed to be putting forth an elaborate act, as if his every word and motion were the product of a performance, meant for an audience, even when she had been the only spectator. But was that not what she was doing? Putting forth an act before him? The difference was that she had a reason. Lord Ramsbury simply was not capable of being genuine.

Annoyance flared inside her. She couldn't imagine ever marrying a man like him. She pitied the woman that he would one day marry, grateful it wouldn't be her.

Looking down at the box in her hand, she gave a soft smile. "From what I have seen of Lord Ramsbury I know him to be a very good man, indeed."

"Then I approve with all of my heart," Uncle Cornelius said with a chuckle. "But you did not answer my question. Who is the man that has caught Harriett's eye?"

Grace looked up, unable to stop her smile. "Mr. William Harrison. Do you know of him?"

Her uncle gasped in his dramatic way, his chest swelling with the inhalation, spreading his waistcoat buttons even wider. "You cannot be serious, my dear! I have been wishing for Harriett to court Mr. Harrison since they were children. He has become such an agreeable man."

Aunt Christine cleared her throat, a smile threatening her prim expression. "As have I. I daresay they are a perfect match."

Grace couldn't stop her squeal. She clapped her hands together, bouncing on her toes. "I knew I could not be the only one who felt this way. But I must be candid. Harriett is not interested in courting Mr. Harrison."

Uncle Cornelius frowned. "Why ever not?"

"You must consult Harriett for an answer on the subject. I do not understand it." Grace smiled at the thought of Harriett's dismay when Uncle Cornelius and Aunt Christine would begin expressing their endorsements of Mr. Harrison too.

Her smile quickly fled when she remembered that Lord Ramsbury would be paying her another visit the next day. Blast it. What did he have planned this time? She hoped it would be short. She didn't know how many more coy smiles she could bring to her face without breaking her act. For a man that she once decided to never see again, she was seeing him quite often.

But all she needed was his proposal. The day he proposed she could bid him farewell forever. It would be a glorious day, indeed.

If it ever came, of course.

With the dread of seeing Lord Ramsbury, Grace had been unable to sleep. She awoke the next morning, her hair disheveled, her eyes swollen, but with her focus increased. When she saw Lord Ramsbury that day she would need to ensure his affection and secure a proposal for herself. She could not carry on with her exhausting act any longer.

Leaping from her bed, she readied herself quickly without waiting for assistance, choosing an ivory morning dress. She and Harriett had come to share their mother's maid, for her parents had dismissed much of the household when their finances had been under pressure a few weeks previous. Her parents would not speak of the distress in clearer terms, leaving Grace and Harriett in the dark. Their pin money had been decreasing as well. She wondered if losing their pin money altogether was a possibility. If that happened then Harriett's incentive in their bargain would be nonexistent.

After securing her hair in a knot at the crown of her head, she walked down the staircase toward the library, hoping to find a book to distract her from her racing thoughts. She assumed Lord Ramsbury would be calling on her in the afternoon once again, so she would have time to prepare herself more fully before his arrival.

As she reached the base of the staircase, she found Harriett standing in the dark of the adjacent hallway, her ear pressed against the door of their father's study.

"Harriett," Grace whispered as she moved down the hall. If her sister was caught eavesdropping on their father's private conversation, she would be in dire trouble.

Her sister jumped, moving away from the door. She put a finger to her lips, eyes wide, motioning with her other hand for Grace to retreat to the entry hall.

Grace frowned, walking closer to the door. "What are you do—" Harriett slapped her hand over Grace's mouth, pulling her in the opposite direction with surprising force. Struggling to free herself, Grace scratched at Harriett's arm, pulling her face away from her sister's grip.

"What are you doing?" Grace's voice echoed loud under the tall ceiling.

Harriett's eyes grew wide. "Hush!" she whispered. "Lord Ramsbury is in the study with Papa."

Grace's stomach flipped. "Truly?"

"Yes." Harriett crossed her arms, glancing to her left down the hallway. "I was able to overhear a small part of their discussion."

"What did you hear?" Grace's thoughts spun too quickly to comprehend each individual one.

"He is requesting your hand in marriage."

Grace's jaw came unhinged, falling open in astonishment. "You cannot be serious."

"Do I appear to be jesting?" Her sister's voice came out dull, dripping with irritation. She certainly did not appear to be jesting.

Grace gasped, covering her mouth with both hands. "I cannot believe that he would already propose. Perhaps I am more skilled than I thought." She let out a quiet squeal. "You must admit that I am indeed an expert in romance, and that you will now begin courting Mr. Harrison."

A look of intense worry overtook her sister's features. Grace rarely saw her so uncollected. "I cannot believe it either," she whispered. "You have managed to effectively romance Lord Ramsbury. I never thought it possible." Her fingers fiddled with the ribbon at her waist, a rueful scowl touching her forehead. "Would you consider only taking my pin money and sparing me the misfortune of courting Wil—Mr. Harrison?"

Grace frowned. "That was not part of our wager."

"Please, Grace." She begged with her eyes, and Grace wondered if she would fall to her knees.

"Absolutely not. That is the only reason I have endured Lord Ramsbury's company these last two days. The wager *was* your idea, after all."

Harriett grumbled something intelligible under her breath, smoothing back her golden curls. "I cannot marry a man of little fortune. At least you have a perfectly eligible and wealthy man in the study that wishes to marry you."

Grace shook her head in revulsion. "No. I could never marry a man I do not love. Or even *tolerate*. At least you will find love as a result of our wager. You will have Mr. Harrison soon."

Harriett let out a long sigh of exasperation, dragging her nails down her cheeks. She seemed to decide against protesting, knowing the effort to be futile, for Lord Ramsbury was about to propose.

*Lord Ramsbury was about to propose.*

"How shall I respond?" Grace asked, panic rising in her voice. "A simple 'no?' Or shall I offer him a thorough explanation of my reasoning? That would be much more satisfying."

Harriett held onto her expression of frustration for the shortest moment before her eyes brightened in mischief. "No, you mustn't offer him any explanation. It will be far more tortuous if you make him wonder."

"Papa will be disappointed when I reject him." Grace glanced at the closed door of the study, feeling as if a brood of hens had begun running in circles within her stomach.

"He will understand. You need only explain that you do not find Lord Ramsbury amiable, and Papa will express his firm accord, and assist you in finding a better match. It is Mama you must be worried about. She will claim that your books have given you unrealistic hopes."

Grace nodded, the nervous fluttering of her stomach never ceasing. Her mother would certainly be distressed with Grace's rejection. She always did blame Grace's lack of interest in the men of Brighton on her reading. It was not that Grace was too selective in her choice of a husband, in fact, she had narrowed her list of requirements to three items. She wanted a man that was kind and honorable, one that could make her laugh—laugh until her sides ached and tears pooled in her eyes—and a man that set her heart racing—that occupied her thoughts when they were apart, and brought a smile to her face at the mere thought of him.

The man that waited in the study did not cross any of these items off her list. Well, at least not entirely. Lord Ramsbury did set her heart racing, but only because she *used* to fancy him. Old feelings were not easily disposed of.

Harriett tugged on Grace's arm, pulling her away from her contemplation. "Now, let us make a place in the drawing room with Mama and prepare her for the news. When Lord Ramsbury requests a private audience with you she will be quite shocked. But not as shocked as she will be to hear you reject him."

With one more glance at the closed door of the study, Grace followed Harriett through the entry hall and toward the drawing room. She couldn't comprehend that in a few short minutes Lord Ramsbury would be alone with her, expressing his desire to make her his wife. Two days? She had never heard of a man proposing after two days.

And she would have never predicted Lord Ramsbury to be the first.

"Grace, what is the matter?" her mother asked as they entered the room, her hands freezing around her knitting needles.

Grace's mother had a keen sense for the emotions of her daughters, as if she were experiencing them for herself. It had always astonished Grace that her mother could detect her unrest from one quick glance. She did not always care, but she always noticed.

"Lord Ramsbury is here," Grace said.

Her mother's mouth opened in surprise. "He cannot possibly plan to—"

"Propose?" Harriet said. "Yes, I believe he does."

"How extraordinary." Her mother flung her knitting to the opposite side of the sofa, standing to meet her daughters in the center of the room. The skirts of her green taffeta gown rustled loudly with the swift motion, adding to her flustered aura. Her brown eyes glowed with pride as she touched Grace's cheek. "Oh, my dear Grace. You will be a lovely bride. Are you certain you wish to marry him? Heavens, just weeks ago you were speaking of your distaste for the man."

Harriett stifled a laugh, masking it with a polite cough.

Grace searched for a proper response, unsettled by the tears of delight in her mother's eyes. "I am not certain, Mama. This does all seem rather sudden." She chewed her nail, hoping to give her mother some indication of her pending refusal.

"Sudden, yes. But quite fortuitous."

The door clicked open behind them. Grace jumped,

her pulse racing as she turned toward the doorway. Her father stood under the frame, nearly filling the space with his broad shoulders. His dark hair, speckled in gray, nearly brushed the top of the doorway as he entered. Lord Ramsbury was a robust man, but compared to her father he fell short. Grace wondered if Lord Ramsbury had been intimidated to meet with him that morning.

All to receive a rejection.

Her father cleared his throat, his stoic expression never failing. Lord Ramsbury appeared behind him in the hall, meeting Grace's eyes with clear admiration. She had to look away. There would be no need for her act to continue.

"Lord Ramsbury wishes for a private audience with Grace," her father said, stepping away from the door, allowing Lord Ramsbury to enter and her mother and Harriett to exit.

Grace swallowed, her throat dry. Lord Ramsbury took three slow paces toward her, his deep-set eyes staring into hers. His dark blonde hair shone golden against the morning sunlight as it filtered past the drapes, his deep blue waistcoat bringing depth to the color of his eyes. She didn't notice her father's exit until the door clicked shut, leaving her alone with Lord Ramsbury.

Her heart thudded as he approached, stopping just one pace away. She focused her gaze on the dust motes that floated in the air near the window, counting to ten in her mind as she awaited his words. His voice, low and deliberate, cut through the silence. "Miss Grace, I—"

"No." She looked away from the floating dust, holding his gaze with effort.

He stopped, a scowl marking his brow. He exhaled in a failed attempt at a laugh. "Pardon me? You did not allow me to finish. I—"

"You do not need to finish, my lord." She offered him a smile. "I will not force you to waste your words of fondness on me any longer. If you mean to offer a proposal of marriage, you must understand that my answer is no. I will not waste your time."

She waited for the look of disappointment in his expression, but all she saw was intense surprise. "No?"

"An emphatic no, my lord."

He blinked, his brow tightening. He pinched the bridge of his nose, squinting his eyes shut. Grace watched him, willing her expression to remain unaffected by her satisfaction. He stood there for a long moment in silence before his eyes opened, a flash of blue. "You are serious?"

She nodded, pressing her lips together. To emphasize her disinterest, she wandered to the sofa, taking up her mother's knitting needles. He would be shocked by her rudeness, to be sure. *Let him be shocked. Let him think me rude.* Grace wrapped the wine colored yarn around the needles, soaking in the silence she had stricken Lord Ramsbury with. It was quite enjoyable.

He gave a hard laugh of disbelief. "Why, pray tell, do you refuse?"

Her mind raced in search of a response. She could think of many reasons, but decided to make him wonder as Harriett had suggested. Shrugging one shoulder, she continued with her knitting, adding a row of loops to the shawl her mother had been constructing.

Lord Ramsbury's boots clicked quickly against the floor, and she looked up just in time to see his hand reach down and steal the yarn and needles right from her grasp.

She glared up at him, no longer attempting to appear polite. She jumped to her feet and turned toward the nearby window. It was covered almost completely in dark greenery from outside, only a hint of the nearby gardens peeking through. "If you think stealing my knitting will make me inclined to provide you with an explanation, you are mistaken, my lord."

She grinned before realizing that Lord Ramsbury would see her triumphant smile reflected clearly on the darkened glass of the window.

He stepped closer—she heard the rustle of his movement.

Mending her expression, she turned to face him, shocked to find him so close. He crossed his arms over his chest, his eyes narrowed. She leaned against the windowsill, hoping to put more distance between them, but it only seemed to encourage him to move closer.

"My lord—"

"Why do you refuse?" he repeated.

Vexation surged within her. She reminded herself that she was no longer required to act her part. "Why do you find my refusal so shocking? You cannot expect every woman you meet to fall madly in love with you."

As her words echoed in the room, harsh and loud, he stared down at her as if she were a foreign creature. "I didn't expect that you *loved* me. I thought you might agree to marry me because you sought the honor of my title."

"There would be no honor in marrying you."

The confusion intensified in his brow, and he muttered illegible words under his breath. "I'm afraid I do not understand."

"I think my answer was very forthright," she said, giving him her sweetest smile.

"If you are so put off by my offer, then why did you behave so…"

"So much like you?"

Annoyance flared in his eyes and his jaw tightened. Grace studied his face. He did not show any sign of sadness or dejection as she imagined a broken-hearted man would appear. It seemed she had been correct in assuming she had only been his next flirtation—he did not have any true feelings for her. Then why did he come to propose at all? It didn't make sense.

"To which behavior of mine are you referring?" he grumbled.

"Your complete disregard for the feelings of the women you pursue. Your senseless flirtation and impudence." Grace clamped her mouth shut before she could say more.

Lord Ramsbury sucked in his cheeks, shaking his head to himself before tipping his face down closer to hers. Her breath hitched, sending her heart into an allegro. Why did she let him affect her composure? She was not sixteen any longer.

Determined to escape, she took a step to the side, toward the nearby sofa. He stopped her, planting both his hands against the window on either side of her arms. She scowled up at him, a stark contrast to her previous smiles.

"Was your receipt of my attention only an effort to spite me?" he asked, astonishment in his eyes.

Grace sighed, crossing her own arms. She couldn't admit it, no matter how badly she wanted to. "Please, do not flatter yourself. I was simply enjoying a meaningless flirtation, just as you enjoy spending your days. As a man, your reputation would never suffer from it, but as a woman, mine very well may. I thought to flirt with you would be harmless. I never thought you would offer a proposal at all."

"I never *did* offer a proposal. You didn't allow me to

speak." He frowned. "Why did you assume I would never propose to you?"

"Let me away from the window and perhaps I'll answer." Grace gave a deliberate glance at his arms, trapping her more near to him than she ever would have liked. Or at least that she *told herself* not to like.

He dropped his hands, letting them fall at his sides. He raised his eyebrows for her to continue.

She stepped away from him, moving to a place near the pianoforte several feet away. "To propose to a woman would imply that you intended to marry her. To marry a woman would imply that you intend to love that woman, and that woman alone, for the remainder of your life."

He leaned against the wall, a weary look in his eyes. "I'm aware of what it means to marry."

"Are you aware of what it means to toy with the feelings of another? I hope I have shown you the suffering it can bring."

He laughed. "Do you think you have toyed with my feelings?"

Grace had not expected him to laugh. She fiddled with the fabric of her skirts, willing herself to appear confident. "Did I not?"

"No."

Grace's stomach fell. "No?"

He smirked. "An emphatic no, Miss Grace."

Anger boiled in her chest, heating her cheeks. This was not the victorious moment she had anticipated. Lord Ramsbury's confusion had quickly transformed to amusement, and she had not intended to *amuse* him. But she still didn't understand why he had taken his acquaintance with her so far if she was simply a game to him.

"Then why did you propose?" she asked.

"First explain why you led me to believe you welcomed my proposal."

Grace blew out a puff of air. "You will think little of me, my lord."

"I already do."

She glared at him, his words stinging deep within her. "I will not explain it all to you. To put it simply, I was involved in a wager with my sister that required that I gain a proposal of marriage from you."

He raised his brows. "Was it required that you decline?"

She scoffed. "That was entirely my decision."

Lord Ramsbury's pride flared, visible in the annoyance that covered his face. "Do you realize the living you are declining?"

"Yes. I also realize the sort of man I am declining."

His expression shifted, real hurt flashing in his eyes. Grace's heart pinched with guilt at the sight of it. She hadn't meant to speak so freely.

"You do not know me," he said finally. "What convinced you to believe that I am so unworthy?"

Grace had imagined herself telling him so many times—the satisfaction she would find in bringing all the faults of his character to his attention. But as she stood before him now, she couldn't find the words.

"We have met before," she said, her voice hardening. "You knowingly toyed with my emotions and then abandoned me."

He squinted at her face, recognition flashing in his eyes. "You did look familiar. I was certain we had met but could not place the moment."

"The Livingston's summer ball, three years ago. A young girl does not forget such careless treatment."

"Well, that is certainly obvious."

Grace gasped, planting her hands on her hips. "Have you no apology to make?"

He shrugged, the devil-may-care grin on his lips infuriating. "I cannot blame myself for pursuing you those years ago, not if you were by any measure as beautiful as you are now."

She ignored his comment, unwilling to believe any word of flattery he spoke. "For one evening, you led me to believe I was the most important woman in the ballroom. You led me to believe I had an opportunity to court the future Earl of Coventry, to step into society in such brilliant light." Grace stopped her words there. She was not going to admit that he had haunted her thoughts and dreams for months, his devastating smile and blue eyes never leaving her mind. Or that she had told almost every one of her acquaintances that Lord Ramsbury had claimed *three* of her dances, only to receive their ridicule when he never acknowledged her again.

"For two days you led me to believe you wished to marry me," he said. "Is that not a greater offense?"

"But your heart was not affected."

"You did not know that until today."

"And so my question arises once again. Why did *you* wish to marry me?"

He rubbed his forehead, leaning heavily against the wall. "I must marry before my father's illness claims his life, or I will be disinherited."

Grace could scarcely believe his words. Lord Ramsbury was to be disinherited? He had been the highly anticipated Earl of Coventry for his entire life. Every person that entered Brighton knew of him. His place in society relied on that forthcoming title, and surely his livelihood relied on his fortune. But there was one question that still lacked an answer.

"Why did you choose me?"

He shrugged. "You were a painfully simple target, what with your intense... interest in me."

"False interest."

His teeth gritted. "I cannot believe that it was entirely false. You said that you once fancied me."

"It is astonishing how much one's opinion can change over time."

Lord Ramsbury opened his mouth to speak but seemed to change his mind. His gaze, heavy with frustration, met hers for a long moment before he turned, exiting the room without another word. Grace watched his back until the door closed firmly behind him.

Her shoulders relaxed; she hadn't realized how tense her posture had been. Her mind raced with the reality of what she had just said and discovered. Lord Ramsbury had only pretended to be interested in her in an attempt to keep his inheritance. She had only pretended to be interested in him to win a wager. Her heart sunk a little at the realization. Though she despised him, she had fancied the thought of him genuinely caring for her. But as a reader of many works she understood the significance of irony.

When she heard the front door of the house signal Lord Ramsbury's exit, she sat down on the sofa. With a heavy sigh, she snatched up the knitting Lord Ramsbury had so rudely stolen from her grasp, awaiting her family's reprove. If perchance they had been listening from the hall, she would be in severe trouble.

# Chapter 6

Edward had never been a skilled swordsman. But he had never attempted it after being harshly rejected by a woman, a fate which had now befallen him twice.

*Twice.*

His arm came down with unexpected speed, his epee making direct contact with Henry's, the metal scratching as they collided. Edward advanced on his brother, fighting with renewed strength and skill. He could hear Henry's laugh of disbelief as Edward managed to disarm him, pressing the blunt tip of his epee against the rapid rise and fall of his brother's chest.

Henry pulled off his mask, his eyes wide and his face beaded with perspiration. He wiped his forehead with the back of his hand. "I never thought I would see the day that you conquered me."

Edward lifted his own mask, catching his breath. His

hair stuck to his forehead, and he pushed it away, lowering his epee. "And I never thought I would see the day that Miss Grace Weston rejected my proposal. I was certain Miss Buxton's rejection would have been the last and only."

Henry shook his head, a broad smile breaking over his face as he crossed the room for his cup of water. "Forgive me if I find it amusing. Both you and Miss Grace were acting with some measure of deceit toward the other. But in the end, she won her wager and you are still without a wife." He fell into laughter.

Edward scowled, taking an angry swig from his own cup. He found himself wishing the cup contained something stronger than water. "I cannot simply let her claim that victory and leave me without mine." It had been a full day since Edward proposed to Miss Grace, and he had spent every moment since trying to understand her aversion to him. It seemed he wasn't as charming as society had taught him to believe. His pride had been bruised to say the least, and it would vex him for months. He simply *couldn't* be rejected a second time. He refused.

Henry raised both eyebrows with a laugh. "Do you still wish to marry her?"

Edward considered the question for a long moment. "Yes, and I plan to."

"Please do explain." Remnants of Henry's laughter still crept into his voice, shaking his words. "Is it that you can't fathom the notion of a woman being resistant to your charm?"

"She made a fool of me, Henry. She is a wicked, spiteful woman, but yes, I still wish to marry her."

Henry stared at him for a long moment, his brow scrunching. "Why?"

A smile crept over Edward's lips. "I enjoy a challenge."

"This is a marriage, not another game of whist. It should not be taken lightly."

Edward hardly heard his brother. "What did I do wrong the last time with Miss Buxton? I was not persistent." He paced the floor. "I asked her once, she refused, and I have regretted it for almost a year. I should have asked her again. I should have romanced her a little longer. I know I could have changed her mind."

Henry stared at Edward as if he were mad. "Would it not be easier to choose a new woman to pursue, one that does not *despise* you? Do you even like Miss Grace at all? You did just call her wicked and spiteful."

Edward stopped his pacing, coming to stand in front of his brother. He clapped him on the shoulder, new enthusiasm pulsing within him. "To choose a new woman would mean I was accepting my defeat. Again. No, never again. Miss Grace is going to fall in love with me. I am going to make certain of it."

"Are you forgetting that you will still have to *marry* her?" Henry asked in an exasperated voice.

"And so I will win back my inheritance. If I must marry a woman I don't love, I don't care who that woman is, even Miss Grace Weston will suffice. Do not try to stop me, brother. My apologies, but you will never see your day as the Earl of Coventry."

Henry laughed, rubbing his forehead. "I am glad to see your tenacity has returned."

"And you shall never see it leave me again." Edward winked, elation building in his lungs as he drew a heavy breath. He had convinced himself to attempt a seemingly impossible task. Miss Grace was determined not to love him. He was determined to change her mind. When he was through with her she would be begging *him* to marry her. But he would need to approach it differently this time. His forward flirtation did not affect Miss Grace the way he had seen it affect other women. Her resistance to him was pure motivation.

"No woman rejects Lord Ramsbury and comes away unharmed," Henry said with a chuckle.

Edward raised one eyebrow. "What is so harmful about a bit of romance?" Giving his brother one final clap on the shoulder, he turned on his heel, bursting through the doors of the ballroom. He would need to freshen his appearance before beginning his earnest pursuit of Miss Grace.

"Edward!" A little voice reached his ears from down the hall. He turned to see his young sister Juliet, standing in the doorway of his father's bedchamber. Juliet had just turned ten years old the month before, and had spent the last fortnight with their cousins in Henfield.

"Juliet! I have missed you." Edward smiled, walking forward to meet her. "Did you enjoy your time in Henfield?"

Juliet shrugged one shoulder, a look of deep contemplation entering her sharp blue eyes. "I wished Papa could have come with us."

Edward's heart stung at the grief that contorted her small features, the tears that balanced on her lower lashes. Their father's illness had made the greatest impact on Juliet. He bent over to be closer to her height, placing one hand on her shrugging shoulder. "Would you like me to read you a story? And then you may tell me of all your adventures in Henfield."

Her eyes flicked back through the doorway, settling on the bed where their father lay, deep in slumber.

"When we are finished we may return here and tell

Papa of your adventures as well," Edward said. "But for the moment he must rest."

Juliet nodded, her golden curls bouncing atop the puffed peach sleeves of her day dress. She grasped his hand and he straightened to his full height, his muscles aching from his recent match with Henry.

"Mama spoke to Papa this morning," Juliet said as they walked to the library. "He said that you were going to marry soon." She threw him an inquisitive glance, her pale eyebrows contracting.

"Indeed, I am." He smiled down at her. Even Juliet appeared surprised.

"Who is the lady?"

He hesitated before stopping himself. If he was going to undertake such an arduous task, he needed to have full confidence in his ability. "Miss Grace Weston."

A small smile pinched Juliet's lips. "Is she beautiful?"

"Yes."

"How beautiful is she?" His sister stared up at him, hope and excitement shining in her expression.

He thought of Miss Grace and her fierce brown eyes, sweeping lashes, and rich brown hair. He had found it shocking that such a pretty and seemingly mild woman could be so devious. Since the day before, when she had expressed her aversion to him, he had found her to be immensely more fascinating. He couldn't explain it, nor could he rid his thoughts of her scowling face.

Edward knew his sister to be fond of clear description, so he chose his words carefully to describe Miss Grace. "She is as beautiful as a sun setting over the ocean, a night sky filled with stars, or a rose in full bloom."

Juliet's smile grew and her eyes came out of focus, as if trying to picture the woman in her mind.

A set of feet clicked on the marble behind them. "And who might you be speaking of, Edward?"

He turned, meeting the rapturous gaze of his mother. Her smile spread even wider than her daughter's, her fine wrinkles and age the only difference between their faces. "I was told you were seeking a wife, but could not believe it."

"When faced with a stipulation like the one Father gave me, I had little choice in the matter." Edward said, keeping the bitterness from his voice. He realized a smile still lingered on his face, brought to his attention by his mother's intense study of it.

"I see that I was right in desiring for you to marry," she said. "This woman you speak of has already had a positive effect on you. I have not seen a smile like that for months. What is her name?"

He couldn't give Miss Grace any credit for his elevated mood. Could he? It was true that he hadn't found any purpose in his life for months, and now he had a goal to work toward. She had given him that much, but his reason for smiling was less honorable than his mother hoped. He smiled at the idea of Miss Grace falling in love with him—falling prey to her own trick.

"Her name is Miss Grace Weston. But we are not engaged yet," he reminded his mother.

"Well, the woman would be foolish to refuse you."

He gave a pained smile. "Yes, she most certainly would."

"I do look forward to meeting her."

"And you shall, very soon." He hoped it were true.

"How wonderful. I did miss you, Edward." His mother's eyes shone with tears as she stared up at him. She had only been away for a fortnight, yet she acted as if she had not seen him for much longer than that. "I have missed seeing your firm mind at work. Nothing has excited you for a long while. When I meet this Miss Weston, I will have much to thank her for." She patted his cheek, smoothing her hand over it. "And if she was what compelled you to shave, then I will have even more gratitude to express."

Edward tore his face away from her hand, laughing. "You have Henry to thank for encouraging the shave."

Juliet giggled. "I did not like your beard."

He gasped, rubbing his jaw. "How dare you insult it?"

"I may insult it now because you cut it off."

"Shall I grow a new one?"

"No," his mother and sister said in unison.

If his pride had been bruised before it was now trampled. "Very well. My face will remain bald for what remains of my existence. Does that please you both?"

Juliet nodded, giggling behind her hand. Edward's mother gave him a loving smile before offering her approval as well.

"I will not subject myself to your insults any longer." He winked at his mother before pulling Juliet along by the hand. "We will be in the library."

"May we take a walk instead?" Juliet asked. "I want to play with the sand by the ocean."

"Shall we read our story by the sea instead?" he suggested.

Juliet gave an eager nod.

"Remember to behave as a proper young lady, Juliet," their mother said as they retreated down the hall. "Keep your dress pristine. We have been invited to a dinner party this evening."

"Only if Edward doesn't throw sand at me," Juliet said, her words disappearing behind her giggles.

Edward laughed at his mother's look of dismay.

"Has this happened before?" she asked.

He exchanged a glance with his sister. "Yes, but Juliet threw seawater at me first."

"Edward Beaumont, you are six and twenty," his mother gasped. "I would hope for more maturity from you."

"Is that not why you seek a wife for me?"

She raised a scolding finger at him, a smile breaking through her censure. "Please return by five o'clock. Our dinner invitation came by a man of your acquaintance. Cornelius Arnold, the Baron of Hove."

Edward didn't recognize the name. But it didn't surprise him, considering that he had forgotten the time he had first met Miss Grace. When she had mentioned it, he did indeed recall dancing with a beautiful young lady at the Livingston's ball. But after learning the true nature of Miss Grace's spiteful character, he couldn't say he regretted snubbing her afterward.

"We will return in time to dine with Lord Hove," he assured his mother.

He led his sister down the hall to the library, throwing his mother one last smile as they passed. Juliet chose a short children's story from the shelves of the library before they left the house, stepping into the warm spring air.

Clemsworth was located very close to the ocean, the scent of the sea wafting up through the breeze. Edward could feel the moisture of minuscule droplets of water in the air, and if he concentrated, he could almost taste the salt of the sea. He had spent his entire life in Brighton, only leaving for brief periods of time. As someone who had always had the ocean nearby, to be distant from it made him feel as if he were missing part of his soul.

Juliet let go of his hand as they approached the sloping

bank that led down to the even sand. Waves peaked in the distance, frothing with tiny white bubbles, growing until they reached the shore then crashed gently over the smooth sand. This side of the beach rarely saw visitors. It was far enough from the center of town—from the pavilion and social assemblies.

"May I go closer to the water?" Juliet asked.

"Only if you promise that you will not splash it at me."

She giggled, picking up her skirts as she took careful steps into the shallow water. She took another step, and another, until the water soaked into the hem of her skirts.

"Juliet, Mama will be fit to be tied if I allow you to ruin your dress." He walked behind her. She turned her face toward him, a mischievous smile on her lips as she skimmed her hand over the water, sending a spray toward his face. He gaped at her as the water dripped down his hair, falling into his eyes. The salty water burned as he blinked it away.

She laughed, terror entering her gaze as he scooped up a handful of wet sand.

"No!" Her laughter verged on hysterical as she backed away from him, her wet skirts dragging behind her.

He scooped up another handful, the dirty water soaking into his white sleeves. He gave her a teasing smile. "You should not have thrown water at me. I'm afraid I must have my revenge." He wouldn't actually throw the sand at her, of course. But Juliet did not know that.

She shrieked, covering her face. Edward gave a wicked laugh, advancing toward her.

A gasp met his ears from the path behind them, just as he raised his fistfuls of sand. He glanced back. There stood Miss Grace Weston and her sister, both with looks of severe shock as they watched his display. Juliet uncovered her face, following his gaze up the sandy slope to where the women stood.

Edward dropped the sand, wiping the remnants on his breeches without thinking. He could only imagine how he must have appeared. Juliet had stopped laughing, which only made him appear more guilty of frightening a poor child. What the devil were the Weston women doing here?

Miss Grace uncovered her mouth, fixing him with a look of sheer disapproval before gripping her sister's arm and walking down the bank toward him. She gave him a brief nod of greeting for the sake of propriety. Her eyes darted to Juliet with concern, who stared up at her with clear curiosity.

Edward nodded at both Weston ladies, bringing his gaze back to Miss Grace. Consternation showed in every line of her expression. If he had any slim hope of convincing her to marry him, it was now decreasing by the second.

"Please meet my sister, Juliet Beaumont," he said in a quick voice. "She recently returned from a visit to Henfield. Juliet, please meet Miss Weston and Miss Grace."

Juliet smiled up at the latter, an uncharacteristic shyness entering her expression. "Please stop Edward from throwing sand at me."

He gave a quick laugh, holding up his empty, and rather dirty palms. "I was simply teasing you, Juliet." He found Miss Grace's eyes, hoping to convince her that he was not a wicked elder brother. "We came to the beach to read one of Juliet's favorite stories." He opened his jacket where he had tucked the thin volume, withdrawing it for her to see.

Miss Grace took the book in her hands and studied the

cover. Her eyes grew wide. "*The Horse and The Lady.*" She looked up. "This was my favorite story as a child. I forced my governess to read it to me every morning before I would comply with our lessons." A smile spread over her cheeks and she looked up. His heart momentarily stalled. The smile she wore now appeared nothing like the smiles she had flaunted before. The moment she met his eyes again, her smile faded, as if she were remembering that she hated him.

Feigning disinterest, she placed one hand on her hip, extending the book toward him. "Do you enjoy *The Horse and The Lady* as well, my lord?"

"I read it to Juliet often," he said, taking the volume from her hand. "It is quite fascinating."

She narrowed her eyes at him, as if she had already determined his words to be false.

"Are you the lady Edward is going to marry?" Juliet asked, her head tipped up toward Miss Grace.

Edward gave a hard laugh, stepping in front of his sister before she could say anything else. Juliet peeked around him, gazing up at Miss Grace once again. "You are just as pretty as he said you were."

Miss Grace frowned, her gaze darting between Edward and his sister. "That is very kind of you to say," she said to Juliet. "But I am not marrying your brother. You must have mistaken me for another lady." Her gaze rose to Edward's, a smirk hovering on her rosy lips.

He pinched his eyes shut before glancing down at Juliet, whose brow scrunched with confusion over the trouble she had caused.

He searched his mind for suitable words to explain Juliet's statements but could find none. What was wrong with him? Awkwardness hung in the air between him and both Weston ladies, thick and unrelenting. After a long moment of excruciating silence, the elder Miss Weston tugged on her sister's arm, pulling her gaze away from Edward.

"We mustn't be late," she said in a whisper.

Miss Grace nodded, throwing him one more glance before following her sister back to the path. "Good day, my lord. I hope you enjoy the story, Miss Juliet." She offered his sister a kind smile before sweeping her skirts up behind her, following her elder sister up the bank.

The confidence he had felt that morning transformed to frustration. If Miss Grace had not caught him by surprise he would have been able to appear collected and charming. Why had she chosen to take the path past Clemsworth to her destination? He was never such a stuttering niddicock. *Deuce take it.*

Juliet tugged on his sleeve, and he looked down at her. He pressed his fingertips to his forehead. "Yes?"

"I do not think she wishes to marry you."

He exhaled, long and slow, laughing at the solemnity of Juliet's expression. "Truly? What led you to that conclusion?"

"She looked at you the way you look at cucumber soup."

Edward wanted to laugh, but her comparison was painfully accurate. He despised cucumber soup, and Miss Grace despised him. He fixed his gaze on her as she grew smaller in the distance, engaged in deep conversation with her sister. He wondered what sorts of terrible things she was saying about him.

"Opinions are capable of changing," he said.

Juliet shook her head. "I do not think you will ever like cucumber soup."

"Do you think Miss Grace will ever like me?" He didn't

know why he was relying on the wisdom of a child.

She tipped her head to the side, her eyes rising to the heavens in thought. "No."

Edward gritted his teeth. He was beginning to think Juliet was right, but he refused to allow an awkward chance encounter ruin his opportunity. Miss Grace had smirked at him just now as if she were still winning their game. He would need to change that at once.

He grumbled to himself as Juliet began tracing drawings in the sand, humming an unfamiliar tune. The next time he saw Miss Grace, he would ensure that he was prepared.

# Chapter 7

Sitting in the parlor of Uncle Cornelius's house, Grace awaited the dreaded questioning of her uncle regarding her proposal from Lord Ramsbury. Fortunately her parents still hadn't learned of her wager with Harriett, so when she told them of her rejection of Lord Ramsbury, they were only confused, if not very disappointed that she would not become a countess. But Uncle Cornelius did not yet know of her refusal.

Grace had convinced Harriett to accompany her to their Uncle's house for dinner. The invitation had been extended to their entire family, but their parents were bound by prior invitations.

Unfortunately, Lord Ramsbury's residence of Clemsworth lay directly between Weston Manor and their uncle's home, so it had only been mildly surprising to find Lord Ramsbury on the nearby beach. But to see him chasing after his young sister with fistfuls of wet sand had certainly been a surprise.

"At least we know that Lord Ramsbury genuinely finds you beautiful," Harriett said, crossing her hands in her lap. "Even if he did only *pretend* to be in love with you."

Grace felt her cheeks warm. Her mind had been spinning for the last day, replaying her conversation with Lord Ramsbury in the drawing room over and over. She had won her wager with Harriett. So why did she still feel as if she were losing in an entirely different battle?

"His sister was very young," she said. "She must have mistaken me for another woman."

"I do not think so."

Grace tried to ignore her sister's words, but they twisted and writhed inside her, making her feel things she didn't want to feel. Lord Ramsbury had seemed… different on the beach. His interaction with his sister had been disconcerting at first, but it became clear that he was merely playing a game with her. Much like he had been playing a game with Grace.

She shook her thoughts of him. She had no need to interact with him ever again, so there was no reason to dwell on him any longer. It was Harriett's courtship that would now be at the forefront of their family's attention.

Pulling her lips into a grin, Grace leaned over the edge of the brocade sofa, leaning her chin on her hand as she stared at her sister.

"What are you staring at?" Harriett eyed her with suspicion.

"I am staring at the future Mrs. William Harrison."

With a groan, Harriett covered her face, slumping in her armchair in a most unladylike fashion. "How do you expect *me* to initiate a courtship with him? And three meetings? The public will hear of it and assume a marriage is imminent. My reputation could very well be ruined when I put an end to our courtship after such a long time."

"You will not put an end to the courtship because you will be desperately in love with him."

She exhaled through puffed cheeks. "Grace Weston, you are infuriating."

"*Lord Ramsbury* is infuriating."

Harriett sat up. "Well, it seems the two of you are designed for one another. It is my turn to act as matchmaker."

Grace gasped. "We are not!"

"Ponder over it for a moment. Both of you acted with the intent to deceive the other, and both of you had no qualms about pursuing someone for your own gain. You are both stubborn and prideful and cunning, if not very endearing when seen in the correct light. If Lord Ramsbury were a female, he would be named Miss Grace Weston."

Grace's pride stung, a testament to her sister's words. Was she really as prideful as Lord Ramsbury? Her pride was what ultimately led her to accept Harriett's wager in the first place. She had been unable to accept that her sister didn't see her as an expert in romance, and she had acted with despicable vengeance. Perhaps she was becoming more like Lord Ramsbury than she had ever wanted to be.

For the first time in a long while, Grace acted with a bit of intelligence, choosing not to refute her sister.

She had been a fool of the most foolish sort.

It was fortunate that her courtship with Lord Ramsbury hadn't progressed further than it did. If society had begun to gossip of it, she would have hurt her own reputation while trying to defend her pride and scathe the man that hurt her three years before. Three years was a long time to keep grievances stirring in one's heart. It did awful things to their character. Grace was living proof of it.

Sickened with herself, Grace chewed the nail of her thumb in silence.

Uncle Cornelius walked through the doorway, flustered as he straightened his cravat. With his thin hair sprouting over the top of his head, he resembled the sand reed growing outside by the ocean.

"Our guests will be arriving at any moment." He glanced out the window, his eyes glowing with anticipation.

"Guests?" Grace asked.

"Yes, your aunt Christine and uncle Richard. And… a few others." He gave a heavy sigh, tossing her a grin. "I hoped to surprise you. Will you allow me to do that?"

Her heart pounded. She had learned that her uncle often revealed secrets through his eyes. Whether it was a glow of mischief, a sheen of sadness, or a spark of anger, she knew him to be unable to mask a single emotion he felt. As she stared into his eyes now, she found every sign of mischief, and a gleeful excitement that could only mean one thing.

"I invited your betrothed to dine with us. His mother, Lady Coventry, and a brother and sister will be joining us as well. Lord Coventry is ill, as you know, and was unable to join. My cook has prepared a fine meal of roasted turkey to celebrate your engagement."

A rush of faintness flooded Grace's head, and her vision spun. "You invited Lord Ramsbury?"

No. It could not be true.

"Indeed." Her uncle frowned. "Are you not pleased?"

*No. No. No.*

"Are you unwell, my dear?"

She pressed her palm to her forehead, the sickness in her stomach spreading, contracting the muscles in her legs. She doubted she could stand when their guests entered the drawing room.

To her credit, Harriett came to Grace's rescue. "Uncle, you must know, Grace did not accept Lord Ramsbury's proposal of marriage. To have him join us here will be quite, dare I say… awkward."

"Excruciatingly awkward," Grace added, composing herself enough to speak.

Uncle Cornelius's eyes now resembled saucers, round and glassy. "I see. Oh, dear. Oh, dear." He paced in front of the window. "I cannot turn them away now."

"We will leave before they arrive." Grace jumped to her feet, her cream skirts tangling between her shaking legs. She gave her uncle a rueful smile. "I hope you will understand."

"Of course, my dear. But why did you reject him? I thought you to be well suited to one another."

Grace now understood Harriett's aversion to the overuse of the term *well suited*. Her uncle craved details, and would never let them escape before he received an answer to his question.

"I find him infuriating," she said with a shrug. It was time she learned to be honest.

Uncle Cornelius took her words with great surprise, pressing a hand to his chest. "That is no reason to reject him. Certainly my late wife found me infuriating at times, may she rest in peace. But that did not stop her from loving me."

Grace could not win the argument. Her gaze slid to the window, halting on the carriage that had just stopped on the drive. They were too late to escape. She took to chewing her nails with renewed vigor, enough that Harriett stepped up beside her, gripping her wrist in order to pull her hand from her anxious teeth.

"Fate acts in mysterious ways, sister."

"Please never say that again." Grace's heart lurched in her throat as Lord Ramsbury stepped down from the carriage, lifting little Juliet out behind him.

"Now you understand how I feel when you prattle on about Mr. Harrison," Harriett said with masked spite.

"Hush." Grace turned away from the window, her cheeks flushing. "How is my hair?"

Harriett raised an amused eyebrow.

"Oh, never mind. I don't care what that man thinks of my hair." She crossed her arms, reclaiming her seat on the sofa, returning her attention to her uncle. "Did Lord Ramsbury know that Harriett and I had also received invitations this evening?"

He blinked. "Well, no, I suppose not. I extended the invitation with the intent to further acquaint myself with him, to decipher his worthiness of you. Only after I knew he proposed did I invite your family. His arrival was meant to be a pleasant surprise."

It was a surprise, but not a pleasant one. Grace drew a deep breath, hiding behind the half-drawn drapes as Lord Ramsbury, along with his family, ascended the front steps. She considered throwing herself between the butler and the front door, but her legs refused to move. All she could do was stand with tense shoulders and hope that Lord Ramsbury wouldn't assume she had orchestrated this dinner party when he found her standing in the parlor.

"Do not allow him to see that you are unsettled,"

Harriett whispered as the sound of the front door opening reached them.

"I am not unsettled." Grace's voice came out too defensive.

Harriett didn't appear convinced. Like a loyal sister, she seemed inclined to ease Grace's burden as much as she could. Harriett stepped slightly in front of Grace, hiding her from immediate view as Lady Coventry and her family were announced in the doorway.

Steadying herself, Grace stepped away from the protection of her sister, willing herself to appear more confident than she felt.

Lady Coventry entered the parlor first, her genteel air and pleasant smile providing Grace with a hint of comfort. Her features held curiosity and joy, with blue eyes and delicate features like her young daughter. Her age showed in the silvery strands entering her pale hair, and in the smiling creases at her eyes.

Mr. Henry Beaumont stopped as he noticed Grace and her sister standing there. His brows raised and his gaze slid uncomfortably to his brother as he entered the room.

Grace's breathing came to a momentary halt. Lord Ramsbury had changed his clothing since she had seen him at the beach, choosing a pale green waistcoat and pure white cravat. His hair appeared to have been untouched, mussed and falling over his forehead. Yet somehow the style suited him, a devil-may-care approach to his appearance that few men could execute well.

She realized with dismay how long she had been staring at him. His jaw contracted when his eyes met hers. For the second time that day, he appeared discomposed and surprised at the sight of her. He stayed near the doorway as Uncle Cornelius made introductions around the room.

Her poor uncle had never appeared more uncollected, stumbling over his words of introduction. When he reached Lord Ramsbury, he gestured at Grace, his face contorting in thought over the proper words.

"We have been acquainted," Lord Ramsbury said, his eyes fixed on hers.

"Yes, of course," her uncle stuttered, clapping his hands together. "My sister and brother-in-law will be arriving soon." His anxious gaze traveled to the window, where the couple's gig had stopped in the drive. "Ah! There they are now."

Grace avoided Lord Ramsbury's constant gaze, keeping hers fixed out the window as well, watching Aunt Christine and Uncle Richard as they descended lazily from their seats.

*Hurry!* Grace demanded in her mind, wishing her slothful aunt and uncle could hear it. She couldn't bear the awkwardness of the room any longer. She wished for a fan with which to cool her burning cheeks, the intensity of Lord Ramsbury's stare heating them beyond what was comfortable.

When her aunt and uncle finally entered the house, Grace was glad to hear Uncle Cornelius's hasty introductions. "That is all, then," he said, a sheen of perspiration on his brow. "I believe our first course awaits. Shall we remove to the dining room?"

Mr. Beaumont seemed to understand the awkwardness of the party. His brother had undoubtedly informed him of Grace's harsh rejection. Lady Coventry's expression remained pleasant as she surveyed the furnishings of the room, oblivious to the tension that permeated the parlor. She followed Uncle Cornelius out of the parlor, her daughter in tow. Aunt Christine clutched her husband's arm and marched toward the dining room, ever the eager dinner guest.

Escorted by Mr. Beaumont, Harriett left Grace's side, leaving her to the mercy of Lord Ramsbury.

Grace's heart pounded as he approached her. Where was the fortitude she had felt at her own home when faced with his proposal? It was gone, along with her resolve to hate him. He was her equal in honor of character, just as Harriett had said. If she had no hope for his redemption then she had no hope for her own. She couldn't continue hating him. But that did not mean she had to enjoy his company.

It took her a moment to realize his arm was extended to her. She swallowed past her dry throat, flashing her gaze up to his. She didn't know what she had expected to see on his face, but the possibility of a polite smile had not crossed her mind. She blinked in surprise.

"I did not expect to find you here, nor did I expect Lord Hove to be your uncle," he said, amusement in his voice.

She shook herself of the confusion she felt at his expression. "I did not know your family had received his invitation."

"Why *did* your uncle invite me here?"

Grace tugged at her gloves, seeking a distraction from his unrelenting stare. Why must he look at her so intently? "He assumed that I accepted your proposal and that we were happily engaged." Taking his arm with a tentative touch, she told herself not to notice the obvious breadth of the muscle beneath his jacket. She noticed anyway.

"How wrong he was."

"Indeed."

Lord Ramsbury chuckled, a deep sound that sent unwelcome shivers over her skin. "How fortuitous that I should find you here. Our brief encounter today at the beach was not long enough. I have been eager to see you again."

She scowled. "Have you?" Surely he wasn't serious.

"I must offer my sincere apology."

She stared at the group ahead as they walked, unwilling to look at his eyes. "For what misdeed do you mean to apologize?"

"For all my misdeeds toward you. And there have been many."

She glanced up, the temptation too great. He stared into her eyes with a level of sincerity she had never seen on his face. "Please do name them all," she said. "We have the entire evening."

A smile twisted his lips, creasing his cheek with a dimple. "Very well. First, for my great misdeed at the Livingston's ball. I should not have claimed a dance past the acceptable two dances. I risked your reputation and I toyed with your heart in a most despicable manner. I am sincerely sorry. I hope to have put that man in the past, along with the ridiculous idea that ending my acquaintance with you was wise." A note of flirtation hung in his voice, subtle and jarring.

What game was he playing? "Well, I thought I had ended my acquaintance with you yesterday in the drawing room at my family's residence." Grace cringed. Why could she not simply accept his apology, whether he meant it or not? Her sardonic behavior had become something of a defense in her efforts to keep her heart far from his careless hands.

"I thought as much too," he said. "And I was not pleased with that reality. I do not wish for our acquaintance to end."

She threw him a disparaging glance. "You cannot fool

me, my lord. You confessed your immediate need for a wife, don't you remember? You intend to marry for convenience. You will never trick me into believing you genuinely wish to know me better." She fixed her eyes on his blue ones. "My answer will never change."

A muscle tensed in his jaw as they entered the dining room, frustration hanging over his features.

In his wisdom, Uncle Cornelius placed her as far away from Lord Ramsbury as possible, seating her on the left side of the table end, and him at the right side of the opposite end.

Grace released a relieved breath, settling into her chair. Harriett threw her a concerned glance, to which she responded with a prim smile.

If Grace's interlude with Lord Ramsbury were the product of one of her favorite novels, then he would be genuine in his attachment to her. He would become gallant and brave and honest. But the heroes of her novels were precisely as her mother had told her: unrealistic.

Why did she want Lord Ramsbury to be those things? She had so enjoyed hating him for the last three years. Indeed, her imagination had even contrived him as the villain in many of the stories she read. But whether she liked to admit it or not, her heart was still fascinated with him and his much-too-handsome face. The most exciting heroes were never perfect, at any rate, and heaven knew she did not deserve a perfect man.

But Lord Ramsbury, with his devilish smile, cunning motivations, and secretive blue eyes seemed to be nothing short of a villain.

"Our first course is a favorite of my dear niece, Miss Grace," Uncle Cornelius said as the party took their seats. "We will be served with cucumber soup."

Grace observed Juliet as she turned to Lord Ramsbury, a wide grin on her lips. Mr. Beaumont eyed his siblings, a look of amusement engulfing his usually pleasant expression. Did the family share her love of cucumber soup? They clearly found *something* of the dish to be humorous. The soup was placed around the table, ending with Grace's bowl.

Lord Ramsbury's smile, directed at his young sister, appeared to be the most genuine smile she had ever seen on his face. From her place across the table, she watched as he whispered in Juliet's ear, sending her into a bout of giggles. Their mother threw them a scolding glance, causing Lord Ramsbury to straighten his posture, just a ghost of his previous smile still dancing on his lips.

He caught Grace watching him, throwing her a subtle wink before stealing her uncle in conversation. Grace felt her cheeks warm as she took an angry spoonful of her cool soup.

Throughout the course of the meal, Grace caught the gaze of Lord Ramsbury more often than she liked, most instances entirely accidental. Each time he sneaked a smile at her, or an infuriating wink, she dug her toes deeper into her slippers, her fists curling under the table. She challenged herself to keep her eyes away from him for the entire dessert course, but when the servants placed a dish of compote of pears in front of her, her gaze found Lord Ramsbury, and for the first time that evening, she couldn't help but smile back.

He looked down at his plate, grinning as he pierced a slice of pear with his fork. He lifted it to his mouth, raising his eyebrows as he chewed. Grace looked away and covered her mouth with her napkin, hiding the laugh that bubbled out unexpectedly from her chest.

How humiliating it was to think of her behavior when she had been trying to romance Lord Ramsbury into a proposal. She thought of the day they had spent near the royal pavilion with their elaborate meal.

She corrected her smile, putting on a stoic expression. She couldn't let Lord Ramsbury think she welcomed his secretive glances. If he still thought he could woo her into helping him reclaim his inheritance, he was mistaken. He would need to select a different woman to preserve his precious title.

After the meal, the women removed to the drawing room, leaving the men to their port. Grace and Harriett sat on the sofa, with Lady Coventry and Juliet seated on a fashionable settee across the room. Aunt Christine found her own secluded corner, settling into a broad armchair. Dim evening light touched the room through the windows, and candles had been lit around the space, casting the ceiling in flickering shadows.

Grace eyed the short bookcase beside her and considered selecting a novel to read, if only to clear her mind of Lord Ramsbury. The better option would be to escape to her uncle's grand library, and never be forced to keep Lord Ramsbury's company again. She felt as if she were at the Livingston's ball again, falling for the expiring flattery of an unattainable man.

And all he had done tonight was share a few glances with her.

*Drat.*

She was in a terrible plight.

"Miss Grace," Lady Coventry said, leaning forward slightly. Her voice, tentative and calm, reminded Grace of her own mother's voice, with the exception of the times she scolded her for excessive reading. "I was quite eager to meet you when my son spoke of his growing attachment. Finding you here was a pleasant and unexpected surprise."

Grace shifted in her seat. "Oh. Your son… spoke of me?"

"In the highest regard. I have seen a change in him since he met you, which placed you in my highest regard even before we had the privilege of meeting." Lady Coventry lowered her voice, as if she worried the men would hear from the distant dining room. "My Edward did not smile for months, you see. He took to an unkept style of life, and cared for little in the world."

"He had a beard," Juliet added, her loud voice overpowering her mother's whisper.

Lady Coventry patted her daughter's hand. "Yes. And we have agreed that he is much more handsome without one."

Grace frowned. She wanted to know more of Lord Ramsbury's decline, but worried that to ask would be outside her bounds. She chose her words carefully. "What led him to such a state?"

"He did not shave for a very long time," Juliet said.

The pure disapproval on the young girl's face was enough to make the entire room laugh. Harriett shook the sofa with giggles. Lady Coventry's smile grew to an impossible size, reminding Grace of how Lord Ramsbury had appeared at the dining room table.

"The state of his facial hair was the least of my worries in his regard." Her face grew more serious. Grace could hardly believe Lord Ramsbury's own mother would choose to gossip of him in the drawing room. "He did not share with me every detail," she said, "but I do know that his heart was broken. He has broken a great deal of hearts in his own right, but to have his own so trampled upon… well, it made a blind man see. He changed for the better in his care for innocent hearts, but he shut himself away from the world. He declared to me that he would never marry or fall in love. He became lazy and uninterested in anything. It broke my heart to see him so disheartened. It seemed he would never be himself again. Until you, Miss Grace." Her eyes shone with gratitude.

Lady Coventry's words dug through Grace's skin like needles, stitching threads of sympathy and curiosity. How could Lord Ramsbury's heart have been broken? For a time Grace had doubted he even had one. What part had Grace played in bringing about this change in him? She already knew his attention toward her held alternative motivations. His heart was not involved and neither was hers.

"You mustn't afford me any credit for this change in your son, my lady." Grace said, watching her fingers in her lap as they clasped together. "He hardly knows me at all."

"You have given him a mystery to uncover." Lady Coventry smiled. "I hope you will give him the opportunity to come to know you."

Grace looked up at the doorway just as Uncle Cornelius entered, followed by Mr. Beaumont and Lord Ramsbury. Her heart leapt as Lord Ramsbury's eyes found her. The corners of his mouth lifted, as if her presence and his smile were somehow connected.

To her dismay, the cushion beside her was completely empty. Lord Ramsbury crossed the room to claim it, settling into the sofa, much too close to her. She remembered the moment he had touched her hand in the carriage on the way to the pavilion. She knew he wouldn't dare attempt anything similar here, but she did not intend to give him the chance. Shifting an inch closer to Harriett, she tucked her hands together on her lap, resting them far away from the man beside her.

Setting her jaw and fixing her gaze on her uncle across the room, she ignored Lord Ramsbury's eyes, though she felt them burning on the side of her face. Her uncle had engaged Lady Coventry and Mr. Beaumont in a light conversation, and Harriett sat silently beside her.

"Are you afraid of me, Miss Grace?" Lord Ramsbury's whispered voice brushed her ear, amusement hovering behind it.

She didn't dare glance at his face, knowing how close it would be to her own. "Surely not as afraid as you are of me."

"I am not afraid of you."

"You did not see the expression of terror on your face when I encountered you this afternoon by the ocean. If you had, I daresay you would reconsider that statement."

He chuckled. "I was not *afraid* to see you. I was only afraid that what you saw would lower your opinion of me. I promise that I am not a wicked brother. My sister adores me, in fact."

"My opinion of you could not have sunk any lower." Grace cringed yet again at her merciless stab. He had apologized to her, and she had only continued to spite him. Was *she* becoming the villain? No. She reminded herself that she was likely still a piece in Lord Ramsbury's plan to reclaim his inheritance. He couldn't fathom the idea of losing, and nor could she.

"Has your opinion changed at all?" His whispered voice set her heart pounding. The warmth of his closeness was enough to evoke a lightness in her head. She tossed him a glance from the corner of her eye. His eyes narrowed down at her, a devastating smile on his face as he awaited her reply. She couldn't bring herself to give him the answer he wanted.

"Not particularly," she said.

He laughed, crossing one leg over his knee. She listened to his laughter, unfamiliar with the depth of it. A wayward smile pulled at one side of her mouth.

"Do you not believe me?" she scoffed.

"No," he said, his voice resolute.

"And why not?"

He leaned closer, and she found herself shifting closer to Harriett. "You pretend to hate me, but I know that is not true."

"If I do, why is that of any consequence to you?" Grace whispered. Her uncle didn't seem to notice her prolonged private conversation with Lord Ramsbury. "I do not believe you are fond of me either, no matter what you pretend."

"I find you intriguing, Miss Grace. Even more so since your rejection."

Grace turned fully toward him. "You cannot pretend that my rejection struck you deeper than your pride. If you mean to secure my heart for your own gain, you ought to surrender now."

He crossed his arms, a wry grin on his lips. "I will never surrender."

"Nor will I."

"Edward," Lady Coventry said from across the room, a hint of censure in her voice. If she thought he had been pestering Grace, she was correct. "Would you care to read for us? Lord Hove just finished telling me of the extensive collection of books in his library."

Grace decided she quite liked Lady Coventry. She had saved Grace from a continued conversation with her son, and she seemed to have an appreciation for books.

Lord Ramsbury nodded. "I would be glad to."

Uncle Cornelius clapped, a gesture Grace was beginning to realize he used in an effort to diffuse awkwardness. "Would you show his lordship to the library, Grace? You know the books there much better than I do what with your hours spent there. You may help him select a volume of poetry, perhaps?"

Grace sucked in her cheeks before giving her uncle a stiff smile. The library was on the opposite end of the large house, and the selection of books was indeed expansive. She sensed that Lord Ramsbury was far too pleased with the arrangement.

"Christine will accompany you, of course," her uncle added in a quick voice. Aunt Christine sighed, just loud enough for Grace to hear it from her spot in the room. She stood from her place beside her husband, grunting as if the effort exhausted her.

Grace was relieved that Aunt Christine was accompanying them, but an unwilling and lazy chaperone was almost as ineffective as having no chaperone at all.

Every gaze in the room became fixed on Grace. She withheld her protest of the trip to the library, knowing that to object would only stir up more awkwardness. "Very well. We will be quick."

Lord Ramsbury jumped to his feet, all too enthusiastic about their excursion. Aunt Christine led the way out of the room, mumbling her own objections under her breath. Grace stayed as close to her aunt's heels as possible as they entered the dim hallway.

Lord Ramsbury followed, a definite saunter in his step.

# Chapter 8

Edward smiled in the dark, watching the flustered Miss Grace as she practically trampled over her aunt in an effort to keep herself far away from him. He couldn't believe his fortune in finding her at Lord Hove's residence. The fates were on Edward's side, it seemed. If he had any hope of Miss Grace agreeing to be his wife, he would need to start by convincing her not to hate him, which was proving to be more difficult than he had originally hoped.

Her aunt stopped abruptly, leading Grace to collide with her back. Her aunt turned with a scowl. "You must lead the way, Grace, it is far too dark," she said in a frustrated voice. "I do not know these halls well, and my vision is not what it once was."

Grace tossed her gaze at Edward, an unexplained scowl on her own brow, as if she meant to warn him against coming near her. He took it as pure invitation, of course.

As she slid past her aunt, he followed, catching up to her frantic steps. She threw him a sideways glance, her posture and expression more stoic than his childhood housekeeper Mrs. Knox. But Mrs. Knox hadn't been hiding any secret affection for Edward. Mrs. Knox despised Edward for his wayward behavior as a boy, and she did little to hide her distaste for him. But Edward suspected Grace's behavior to be a defense against him—a defense he intended to break down. She was a different woman than the one he had met in the woods near the assembly rooms. She was bold and headstrong and determined not to like him. Why that made her far more interesting was difficult to say.

"I thought you preferred not to waste your time reading fictional stories," he said, remembering their past conversation. "If that is so, then why did your uncle say you often spend hours in his library?"

She remained silent, watching the floor as they walked. Had she lied about *all* of her accomplishments? As he considered the possibility, he found it to be highly probable. If she was trying to secure a proposal from him, she would have been wise to lie about such things.

"And when we return to the parlor, are you going to perform a number on the pianoforte?" he asked. "You did say you were a skilled musician. You might select a book from the library written in French, since you speak it so flawlessly."

She tore her gaze from the floor, her brown eyes flashing. "As you already know, I was not honest with you. I pretended to be accomplished in those things, just as I pretended to enjoy your company."

He leaned down closer to her as they walked, and she moved faster, putting a greater distance between them and their chaperone. "Ah. And just as you are pretending *not* to enjoy my company at this moment."

"In this instance I do not have to pretend."

"Then stop your charade. We are alone. This is not a parlor game."

"What charade?"

"You are charading as a bitter and cold woman," he said. He stated it as a fact, which only raised her defensiveness.

"And what of yourself?" she asked in an angry whisper. "You are charading as a man in love, but I do not believe it for a moment. You need a wife, one that you know you will never care for, one that will not interfere with the blow that your heart took at that hands of a woman last year. Your mother told me of your plans to avoid love forever."

He sped up, cutting off her progress down the hall as he stopped in front of her. She came to a delayed halt, almost crashing into him just as she had her aunt. She released a huffed breath, crossing her arms as she looked up at him. Far behind them down the hall, her aunt had stopped by a portrait, as if she meant to simply wait for their return.

Edward looked down at Miss Grace, his eyebrows contracting. The moonlight from the windows lining the hall melted into her skin, making it glow white against the contrast of her dark eyes, lips, and hair. For a moment he had a fleeting thought of kissing her, stealing the breath she so willfully used in harsh words against him. For a woman that irked him so much, she was frustratingly enchanting.

"When did my mother tell you these things?" he asked.

"After we left the dining room."

He rubbed a hand over his hair. Why had his mother

betrayed him? Had she meant to give Miss Grace a reason to pity him? Did his mother think it would make him more endearing?

Curiosity burned in Miss Grace's eyes. "You know my feelings toward you. Why do you continue to pursue me? Why do you not choose to pursue a woman that will at least love you?"

Edward took a deep breath. He didn't know the answer. His father could pass from this life at any day, so he had limited time to find a wife. There were still dozens of women that would have him and his fortune gladly. But the smallest part of him was not fond of the thought of Miss Grace marrying another man, just as Miss Buxton had.

And not only for the sake of his pride.

The realization struck him in the chest, and his heart picked up speed as he looked down at her, awaiting his answer with her maddening scowl.

He stepped out of her way, motioning for her to continue down the hall. They continued on their path toward the library. When he offered no response, she repeated her question. He added 'stubborn' to the list of characteristics he had compiled for the new Grace Weston.

"Why not choose a woman who will love you?"

He crossed his arms, not enjoying the vulnerability her question imposed. "I don't believe there is a woman that could love me. She might *pretend*. But all they ever want is my fortune." He threw her a half-smile. "Or to win a wager."

She looked down at the floor as they turned left down an empty hallway, the walls desolate. She was silent for a long moment, calling attention to the sound of their feet on the marble floors. "I'm sorry to have used you so despicably," she said in a soft voice. "I have no excuse for it."

They reached a set of wooden doors on the opposite side of the house from the parlor. Her eyes were cast down in shame, the shadow of her lashes splaying over her cheeks. Was she truly ashamed of her actions? He couldn't decipher which actions of hers were genuine and which were an act. Could she wonder the same thing about him?

He followed her eyes as they traveled down the hall, her aunt nowhere in sight.

"There is nothing to be ashamed of," Edward said. "You were simply a lady who was in want of revenge."

Her gaze shifted up to his, amusement flickering in her brown eyes, twitching her lips with a grin. "There is something that sounds very wrong about that sentence."

"It is all too common, especially when the vengeance is directed at me. My mother is constantly in want of revenge for the trouble I caused her as a child. That is why she told you about my disinclination to love."

"Ah. I see." Miss Grace hid her smile well as she turned toward the library doors. She pushed on the door, and he helped press it open, revealing a much larger room than he had expected. The room was soaked in darkness, illuminated by the filtered moonlight from the room's single window. Bookcases lined the room in the shape of a U, stretching more than halfway to the lofty ceiling. A ladder rested against the far right bookcase, and a round table sat in the center of the space, accompanied by two wide leather chairs.

"Why is it far too easy to imagine you as a troublesome child?" Miss Grace asked, glancing at him over her shoulder.

"Because I am a troublesome man?"

She started to laugh, but stopped when he moved closer, touching her elbow just as the heavy wooden door fell closed behind them. She turned toward him, her firm expression returning as she looked down at his hand on her arm.

"Miss Grace," he said, moving his grip to her hand. She stared up at him, her eyes rounding in surprise. "I do not ask that you love me. I do not even ask that you like me. All I request is that you do not hate me—that you find me… barely tolerable."

She gave a reluctant smile, her gaze fixed downward where he held her small hand tightly in his. "To say someone is barely tolerable is simply a kind way of saying you strongly dislike them," she said.

"But having a strong dislike for someone is not the same as hatred."

Her smile widened, bringing a set of endearing lines to the corners of her eyes. "The two have a difference of a hair's width, my lord."

His gaze became fixed on a strand of her hair, twisting down and falling over her left eyebrow. He lifted his other hand—the one not holding her own—and brushed it aside, tucking it behind her ear. "Well, then, at least I will have made a bit of progress with you."

She immediately cast her eyes down, slipping her hand away from his. It was not a withdrawal of disgust, but unease. He made her feel things she didn't want to feel, it seemed. His heart flipped when she pressed her lips together, marking the left side of her chin with that dimple.

"I cannot say for certain without learning more of your character," she said, turning away from him with a saunter in her step that challenged his own. "Now, come and help me find a book before my aunt wonders what is taking so long. I should hate for her to worry." Miss Grace pulled the ladder closer to the bookcase, climbing up two steps as she carefully studied the shelves, her brow furrowed to read the spines against the dimness.

Edward gripped the ladder, steadying her climb. He blinked up at her. "For what reason could she possibly have to worry?"

She threw him a look of annoyance. "You know perfectly well, my lord."

"I'm afraid I do not." He stared up at her in mock confusion.

She pulled a book from the shelf, blowing dust from the cover. "Then you are far more innocent than I thought you to be." She raised one doubtful eyebrow before leafing open the pages of the book, resting her hip on the ladder to balance.

He chuckled. Of course she would view him as a reputation-destroyer, eager to escape unchaperoned to a dark library to attend to his wicked desires. That was the reputation he had earned. A false one. Yes, he had stolen a kiss or two in his lifetime, but never in the frivolous way gossip had made the public to suspect.

"You are right, I do know," Edward said. "Your aunt is worried because she knows you lured me to this library to steal a kiss from me."

Her eyes flew open as if a ghost had leapt from the pages of the book she held.

"I will not stop you," he said in a low voice. "But do make haste. I know you instructed your aunt to wait in the hall, but she will be getting anxious."

Miss Grace tucked the book she held under her arm, stomping down the ladder. "She stayed in the hall because she is lazy. And I hope to never endure a kiss from you."

"Never? Truly? Not even at our wedding?"

"I will never marry you either!"

He laughed at her rising frustration and obvious discomfort with the conversation. She stopped at the base of the ladder, hugging the small book against her. "I chose a volume of Shakespeare's sonnets. You may select whichever sonnet you would like to read for the party in the drawing room."

He took a step toward her, and he heard her breath catch. She looked down at the floor. He smiled as he stole the book gently from her grasp, amused by her discomfort from his closeness. "I shall choose an extraordinary one."

Her gaze jumped to his. "They are all extraordinary."

"Then I will open the book and read the first one I see."

The library door creaked open, revealing Miss Grace's disgruntled aunt. Her eyebrows pinched together toward the bridge of her nose. "What are you doing in here? Selecting a book should not take so long."

"Not to worry. No reputations have been hurt," Edward said, walking toward the door with a reassuring smile. "I stopped your niece from doing anything dishonorable."

Miss Grace's gasp met his ears from behind, and he threw her a wink over his shoulder. To tease her so mercilessly was not serving his purpose in gaining her favor, but it was all too entertaining.

"Get out here at once," her aunt demanded, withdrawing her fan. She began fanning herself, loose strands of dark hair flying about her face with the artificial breeze. "You are fortunate I checked in when I did. I should have followed you to the room." The woman clutched her niece by the elbow as they entered the hall, leaning close to her ear as if she intended to keep her words secret from Edward. But her attempted whisper could not be hidden among the silence of the house. "Has your reputation been compromised?"

"No, Aunt Christine!" Miss Grace hissed, knowing full well that her aunt's words were far from a whisper. "We selected a book and simply became distracted by conversation. That is all."

Edward chuckled, earning a glare.

They reached the parlor, and Grace dropped herself into her place on the sofa, crossing her arms. He stood at the center of the room with the book of sonnets.

"Ah, Shakespeare. His works are highly favored of my dear Grace," Lord Hove said, sitting forward with excitement. "Which of his sonnets have you selected to read?"

Edward caught Miss Grace's eye from the side of the room. He grinned as he slid his thumb between two pages, letting the book fall open to an unplanned page somewhere in the middle. He skimmed the page, his smile growing. "Sonnet 90. *Then Hate Me When Thou Wilt; If ever, now.*"

"What an... interesting choice," Lord Hove said, his gaze darting between his niece and Edward.

Miss Grace showed every sign of a struggle as she pressed her lips together, fighting the smile that twinged at the corners of her mouth.

Edward cleared his throat, returning his gaze to the book he held, and read from the page.

*Then hate me when thou wilt; if ever, now;*
*Now, while the world is bent my deeds to cross,*
*Join with the spite of fortune, make me bow,*
*And do not drop in for an after-loss:*
*Ah! do not, when my heart hath 'scaped this sorrow,*
*Come in the rearward of a conquered woe;*
*Give not a windy night a rainy morrow,*
*To linger out a purposed overthrow.*

*If thou wilt leave me, do not leave me last,*
*When other petty griefs have done their spite,*
*But in the onset come: so shall I taste*
*At first the very worst of fortune's might;*
*And other strains of woe, which now seem woe,*
*Compared with loss of thee, will not seem so.*

The group applauded as he finished. He turned his gaze to Miss Grace, who simply stared at her lap, twisting her fingers together to avoid looking at him. He gave a quick bow before settling back into the sofa beside her.

"Well done, spoken with such conviction," Lord Hove said.

"Very well performed," his mother agreed. Edward met her eyes, noticing the question that hovered there. She did not miss the smallest of details, so he was certain she had noticed the discomfort in Miss Grace's countenance. And his mother would likely blame him for it.

Henry sat back in his chair, his head tipped to the side as he stared at Edward and the woman beside him, as if he meant to uncover a disturbing mystery. When the rest of the party became distracted with a discussion of Shakespeare's final days, Edward nudged Miss Grace with his arm, a movement so subtle he doubted the room would notice.

"If you are certain you'll hate me forever, say it now, and I will leave you alone," he said in a soft voice, a proper whisper, soft enough to evade even her sister's nearby ears. "Please do not say it once I have fallen madly in love with you." He let a smile enter his voice, but his heart thudded with anticipation. Had he done enough? Would she still deny that she felt anything but hatred for him? *He* felt many things for her. Frustration, annoyance, and impatience were among them. But there was a stirring in his chest, a tingling of his skin and bones, and the urge to smile at her every motion that overthrew it all.

Her brown eyes connected with his, and for a moment, the answer he dreaded burned in her gaze, revealed by the anger there. But it was fleeting, replaced with a flicker of amusement. She looked down at her hands before offering her own whisper.

"Very well. You are barely tolerable."

He sunk back in the cushions with a low chuckle, throwing her a sideways glance. She still avoided his eyes, but an unmistakable grin played at her lips.

"As are you," he said.

Her composure slipped with a quiet gasp, and she turned on him. "I change my mind. You are not tolerable at all."

"I did not think you were capable of changing your mind. You are quite stubborn, you know."

"And you are quite *intolerable*."

He laughed, allowing her the satisfaction of winning the round of verbal sparring. He suspected there would be many more to come.

He hoped there would be.

"Are you otherwise engaged tomorrow afternoon?" he asked.

She gave him a look of disbelief that he had even asked. "Yes."

"What is this activity that demands your time?"

"Reading."

He raised his eyebrows. "Reading?"

"I have a place on my family's property where I enjoy reading each afternoon. I am currently enjoying a tale titled *A Match of Great Consequence*."

Edward heard a sound come from the elder Miss Weston, a huffed breath of disapproval.

"I know it is uncalled for," he said, "but could you perhaps cancel your afternoon visit with your imagination?"

She smirked. "My imagination will be very offended by such an act. So I'm afraid not."

There it was again. Her resistance. If he didn't find it so deuced charming, he might have given up. But he had a different plan. "Do you wish to ever see me again, Miss Grace?"

She released a heavy sigh. "No, but if it is so very important to you… then I suppose I will allow it."

He tipped his head back in laughter, accidentally catching the attention of his mother, followed by Juliet and Henry.

"How generous of you," he whispered, straightening his posture. He sneaked another look at her face. He couldn't recall a time he had been so thoroughly entertained by a conversation with a woman. Miss Grace was proving to be intelligent, witty, and unyielding to the behavior that was expected of her. He couldn't recall the last time a woman had made him laugh either, something he had never expected to happen with her. He didn't want their conversation to end, even with all the prying eyes and listening ears. *Let them listen*. He didn't care.

His mother took Juliet by the hand, moving to her feet. She regarded their host warmly. "This has been a most enjoyable evening. We thank you for your hospitality."

Lord Hove smiled. "You are most welcome. It has been an honor."

As Edward stood to leave, he debated whether or not to schedule a time to see Miss Grace again. He decided against it. How much more effective it would be to make her *wonder* when he would be calling upon her. He smiled to himself. If he was not constantly in her thoughts for the rest of the night, then he would be immensely surprised.

Several minutes later, when he returned to Clemsworth and lay in his bed, he found himself surprised, but for a different reason. Miss Grace and all her snide remarks and rare smiles would not leave his own thoughts.

*Blast it.* He was becoming the victim of his own attack. Worry crept into his mind. If his feelings continued in the direction they were speeding, then it could result in a devastating outcome. If he didn't succeed in winning Miss Grace, and she refused to marry him, she would leave him with scars.

He was on the brink of a cliff. He could surrender now and choose a different woman, one whose rejection would never come, and never sting if it did. Or he could continue in pursuit of Miss Grace, and attempt to keep his heart uninvolved with the endeavor.

Deciding on the second option, he rolled to his back, staring at the dark ceiling. For the first time since his father had announced his stipulation, Edward didn't dread the thought of marrying. He was not fond of it, but a bright fire of possibility burned in his chest as he thought of Miss Grace Weston.

# Chapter 9

The pages of Grace's book were much less interesting than the ever-present image of Lord Ramsbury that dominated her mind. First his blue eyes, then his wide smile, golden hair, and defined jaw. Then came the words he had spoken to her, playing across her thoughts, sparring with the words on the page that vied for her attention.

She set the book down with a heavy sigh. Where was her self-discipline? As the heroine of her own story, she would be losing painfully to the villain as of now. A villain named Edward Beaumont. Allowing him to haunt her thoughts was not an option. But it was so very difficult to banish him from them. She picked at the corner of the cover of her book, chewing her lip. It seemed such charming villains only existed in the real world.

Unfortunately.

Harriett sat on a quilt beneath the nearest tree, shaded

with both a bonnet and a parasol. Her complexion had been blessed with the extra precautions she took, not a line or dot to be seen on her porcelain skin. When they were younger, Harriett would escape out of doors without a bonnet, venturing to the ocean and running through the woods. But now she remained fully shaded, another testament to the change that had occurred abruptly within her. Grace wondered if her sister even remembered how it felt to have the sun warm her cheeks.

"Harriett," Grace said, interrupting her sister's sketching. "Do you think Lord Ramsbury is a liar?"

"I think he is using you for his own designs, yes. But I am not entirely certain of whether or not his feelings for you are real."

Grace had concluded as much herself.

Harriett added to her drawing, deep contemplation in her brow. "He must obtain a wife to keep his inheritance, but that does not change the fact that he wants *you* to be that wife. That must mean something."

"Yes. I suppose you are right." How could Grace blame him for doing whatever it took to keep his inheritance? One did not simply give up thousands of pounds and a place among the *ton* just because of a single obstacle. But her trust wasn't easily won. The moment she took down the defenses around her heart he could desert her once again. He could change his mind at any moment. It could be the day he happens upon a prettier lady in town, or one that finds him more than 'barely tolerable.' He could abandon Grace like an empty glass, just as he had at her first ball.

And to accept his attention after so forcefully declining his proposal was outside her capability at the moment. He would be all too pleased. And she hated to please him.

"Have you found Mr. Harrison in town yet?" Grace asked.

Harriett shook her head hard. "I found his sister at the millinery this morning. She told me he was traveling with his brothers and father until autumn. Something about horses." She shrugged. "At least I will not have to see him until then."

Grace raised a finger at her. "The moment he returns to Brighton, you must fulfill your promise."

"I will," she said through gritted teeth. "But it is not my suitor we ought to be fretting about at the moment. It is yours."

Grace didn't like fretting about Lord Ramsbury. It brought her severe anxiety. "I would rather not. Let us fret about nothing at all, and enjoy a peaceful spring morning without any talk of men." She picked up her book, the romantic story less interesting than it had once been.

When she began to accidentally envision Lord Ramsbury as the dashing hero, she snapped the book closed, deciding that a book of mathematics would better suit her mood and aid her attempt to rid her mind of the odious man. Mathematics would provide her with a different sort of problem to be solved, none involving romance.

Crossing the lawn, Grace made her way to the back door of the house, walking through the hall until she found the library. Her mother had ordered all the books she called 'romantic and unintelligent' to the top shelves of the bookcases, hoping to better keep them out of Grace's hands. She had instructed the servants to use the wooden ladder as kindling for the hearths, leaving Grace with no method of reaching the books she usually sought. But a few months before when Uncle Cornelius had come calling, he had been kind enough to bring a few of her favorites down to a more obtainable reach.

When Grace opened the door, she found her mother and father, both sitting at the table, leaned over an assortment of records.

"Grace!" her mother said, greeting her with a flustered smile. Her father grunted in acknowledgement of her arrival before returning his focus to the parchment he held.

"I heard from Cornelius that Lord Ramsbury was in attendance yesterday at dinner," her mother said, her brown eyes hopeful. "Have your feelings toward him changed? Cornelius seemed to believe that Lord Ramsbury's attachment to you was still very secure."

"Did he?"

"Yes."

"Oh." Grace had been doing well to clear her thoughts of Lord Ramsbury in the three minutes she had spent walking to the library. *So much for that.*

"Your father was quite impressed with him. If his offer still stands, you might consider giving him a different answer. Perhaps?"

Grace shook her head. "No, Mama. I do not intend to marry him."

"Why ever not?" Her mother's gaze slid to the book, *A Match of Great Consequence,* that Grace still held in her hand. A look of deep disapproval entered her mother's eyes. "It is the stories, isn't it? You are too preoccupied with these men of fiction to find merit in a man of flesh."

"That is not true."

Her mother fanned her face with one of the sheets of parchment on the table, anxiety marking a crease between her eyebrows.

Grace felt a lecture coming.

"You have become so immersed in these false worlds that you forget your place in your own world. You are a girl without a dowry of any kind, able to bring little to a marriage, who has rejected the rare opportunity to be a countess, to secure a comfortable living for herself. Do you realize the consequence of this choice you have made?"

"I am not blinded by these false worlds, Mama," Grace said with a sigh. "I learn from them. I learn of different cultures and different people. By reading these stories I am taught by some of the greatest intellectual beings of the past and present. I am finding qualities in the male characters that I would seek in my own companion, and qualities in the heroines that I would seek to develop in myself. It is more educational than you would suspect."

Her mother rubbed her forehead. "Grace. I admire your resolve, but think of what you could accomplish if you applied the time you spend reading to other pursuits. You are a very beautiful girl, and I wish we had the funds to send you to London. I daresay you would be admired by many. But at the moment we have no way to fund a Season, and so Lord Ramsbury is your best option."

Grace refrained from vocally disagreeing with her mother. "If perchance he does extend his proposal again, I will consider it," she said, if only to appease her.

"And you will do nothing to divert it?"

Grace's mother knew her schemes too well. "Nothing at all."

"Good. We have been invited to a spring ball at Pengrave, the residence of the new Marquess of Seaford next week. Lord Ramsbury and his family will likely be in attendance, so I expect you to make an effort there, my dear. Show him that you regret your refusal of him."

"I do not regret it."

Her mother huffed in frustration, turning to her husband for support. He lifted his eyes from the table, a heaviness there that Grace didn't recognize. "You would do well to listen to your mother, Grace. I'm afraid I will be unable to support you and Harriett for much longer. Our debts are increasing, and soon we may have to remove to a smaller home outside of Brighton."

"You cannot be serious" Grace's heart fell, plummeting to her stomach. She had noticed a decrease in their pin money, but hadn't thought much of it.

"I'm afraid I am."

Her mother gave her a heartfelt look. "So you see our urgency. It is not to burden you with a marriage that you will not be happy with, but to ensure that you are well taken care of."

Grace gave a solemn nod. How could she ever leave Brighton? She had spent her childhood here by the ocean.

"Do not allow yourself to be burdened by this, Grace. All we desire for you is happiness," her mother said. She eyed the book in Grace's hand again, disgust sparking in her eyes. "But I would ask that you give that book to me."

What her mother would never understand was that it was books, more than almost anything in the world, that brought her happiness. Knowing her mother would not relent, she set it down on the table. Grace felt as if she were parting from a dear friend, one she had not yet had the privilege to come to know, or to understand. Her mother would never let her see that book again. Perhaps she could sneak to the circulating library in town to see if they shelved a copy.

With a sigh, Grace moved to the nearest bookcase. She found the row of books her governess had once instructed her with. Architecture, French, and mathematics books lined the shelf at her eye level. She selected one and returned silently to the back door of the house.

Had rejecting Lord Ramsbury been a mistake? No. She could never call it a mistake. She knew her heart, and she knew that it had always dreamed of being loved, truly loved, by her husband. She was nothing more than a necessary obstacle to Lord Ramsbury, a device to help him reach his goal. She would never settle for a marriage built on something like that.

Stepping into the warm air, she breathed deeply, inhaling the scent of roses from the nearby gardens, trying to calm her racing mind. The smell never failed to remind her of her childhood, when she and Harriett would pluck roses from the bushes to keep in vases in the room they shared. The servants that cared for the grounds had not been fond of their practice, but she and Harriett had usually managed to evade them.

Grace sneaked to the bush to pluck a rose for Harriett. Careful of thorns, she snapped the stem of a white rose, the petals still wrapped tightly around themselves, as if they were unsure of the endurance of the warmth in the air. She smiled, tucking the rose behind her back as she stepped out from the gardens. She held her new book open in her hand as she walked back to the tree, studying the abundance of numbers on the page with disgust, doubting the wisdom that had sent her back to the library to exchange her book. She detested mathematics.

When she glanced up, her feet stopped of their own accord, bringing her to an abrupt halt.

It was Lord Ramsbury, not Harriett, that now lounged upon the quilt by the tree, spinning the stem of a leaf between his fingers, grinning up at her.

"What the devil are you doing here?" she asked. She covered her mouth with her book, shocked by her own language.

Lord Ramsbury's eyes blinked in surprise and amusement, a rankling smile on his handsome face. Only Lord Ramsbury would find her choice of language amusing and not appalling.

"You might at least pretend you are happy to see me," he said.

She lowered the book, cringing in embarrassment. "I thought we agreed to put a stop to our pretending."

He raised his eyebrows. "Did we?"

"Yes."

"So you would prefer that I *not* pretend I didn't just hear such… improper language escape your mouth?"

Grace released a loud burst of laughter.

He leaned back on one elbow, watching her with a curiosity in his gaze that she didn't recognize. "How extraordinary."

She frowned. "What?"

"Your laugh. It sounds quite different from the laugh you had before—when we played whist and went to the pavilion."

Her giggles subsided. "I'm sorry."

"Do not apologize. I much prefer this one. The other one was…quite terrifying."

She stepped closer, throwing her book down on the grass. Her hands found the familiar place on her hips. "What was wrong with my false laugh?"

"It was the most dreadful laugh I had ever heard." He chuckled.

She shook her head. "Just when I begin to find you tolerable you find a way to change that opinion."

His laughter continued as he picked up her book from the grass, opening it to the first page.

"And you did not answer my question." She sat down on the grass, far away from him, tucking her feet beneath her skirts. She lowered her voice. She did not care what he thought of her. She did not care to be a proper lady at the moment. "What the *devil* are you doing here? And what have you done with my sister?"

He did not appear shocked in the slightest. He gave a pompous smile. "I missed you."

She narrowed her eyes. "Oh, yes. I should have suspected."

"Why do you not believe me?" he asked with a chuckle.

Grace couldn't name the exact reason, simply that she still did not trust him. "You do not possess the most trustworthy face."

"And what makes one's face trustworthy?"

"The absence of a smirk, to begin."

He laughed, a deep and hearty sound. Grace found herself smiling as she watched him, laughing like a child at her accurate description of his face.

"Is that rose for me?" he nodded toward the white bud she had placed beside her on the grass. She had almost forgotten about it.

"It was for my sister. As children we loved white roses."

"Do you still?"

She touched a petal that had already begun to wilt. "Yes. They are my favorite flower." She looked up to find that he had turned his attention back to the book, flipping through the pages.

"I thought you were reading *A Match of Great Consequence*," he said. "And I thought you despised mathematics. Although you told me that during a time when every word that that escaped you was a lie."

"No, that was true. I do despise mathematics." Grace watched as he intently studied the page. "And you said you enjoyed mathematics. Is that true?"

He glanced up, giving a nonchalant shrug. There was a

certain discomfort in his posture and expression, as if he didn't care to admit that he enjoyed it. Grace never would have guessed that Lord Ramsbury enjoyed mathematics, but there were many things she was discovering about him that she didn't know before.

"You may tell me. I will not think less of you for it," she said. "But only if you will not think less of me for my love of books and fictional stories."

He grinned, closing the book in his lap. "Yes, but I have not always loved mathematics. As a child, I despised it. I was terrible at it, and my tutor could not convince me to try." His smile began to fade, pushed into the background by memories and nostalgia. "My uncle, who also lived in Brighton, was very skilled at it. He spent hours helping me learn, until I enjoyed it too. But it was his company I enjoyed more than anything. He taught me to shoot and ride as well. I wanted to be exactly like him when I was grown, give of my time to those that needed it, and make others feel valued. My father couldn't spare a moment for me most days, so when my uncle died five years ago, it felt very much like losing a father."

Grace didn't recognize the seriousness in Lord Ramsbury's eyes, or the pain that settled in his gaze. She didn't like seeing him so serious. She much preferred his teasing over the heaviness in his eyes.

"I am very sorry you lost your uncle," she said. "I cannot imagine losing my Uncle Cornelius. He is also like a father to me. My own father rarely ventures out of his study to see his daughters."

Lord Ramsbury smiled, his eyes softening. "So we have something in common, after all."

"Just not a love of mathematics," she said.

"Or cucumber soup."

Grace laughed. "You don't like cucumber soup?"

"It is the most dreadful thing I have ever tasted." His face contorted in disgust.

"I am telling my uncle that you hated his soup last night, and he will never invite you to dine with him again."

"Good," he said, shivering in dramatic revulsion. "Then I will avoid the risk of being served cucumber soup again."

She couldn't stop her laughter as it bubbled out of her chest, shaking her entire body. Rather than join in her laughter, Lord Ramsbury watched her intently as she struggled through her fit of giggles, shaking with laughter of his own. She met his eyes, unsettled by the admiration burning in them, a sort of quiet awe. *It is part of his act,* she reminded herself.

She stopped her laughter, looking down at the grass as her cheeks warmed. She still felt his gaze, beating down on her face like hot sunlight. "You must miss your own uncle terribly," she said, more comfortable with the last topic of conversation.

"I do. He was very kind to me. Before he died he gave me the book of mathematics which he had used to teach me, with a letter tucked inside. And now my real father is on the brink of death, and his final gift to me was to take away what my birth has promised me my entire life." His expression pinched with bitterness.

Grace traced her finger through the grass. "Unless you marry."

"Yes. But it is unlikely to happen." He sighed, the sound too dramatic and pitiful to possibly belong to Lord Ramsbury.

She looked up, scowling. "Are you attempting to make me feel guilty?"

"Perhaps." His mouth lifted into a slow smile.

"Well, it will not work."

"I suspected so. That is why I have made other arrangements." He stretched out his long legs, crossing his feet in front of him. He cocked one eyebrow in her direction, silently begging her to ask for more information.

"Other arrangements?" Grace's heart fell, and she scolded it for caring. She had turned down his proposal. Of course he would need to find another woman that would not. But why did the idea of Lord Ramsbury with another woman fill her with so much jealousy? The monstrous feeling dug at her stomach with its claws.

He put on a serious expression, as if discussing a matter of business. "Yes, I have selected the eldest Miss Darby to be my wife instead. I'm certain she will have the good sense to marry me."

"Miss Darby?" Grace couldn't hide her disdain. She was only briefly acquainted with Miss Darby, who was more closely acquainted with Harriett, though neither sister would call her a friend. She was a rather odd young lady, always trailing around Brighton with one of her many cats, looking for the next piece of gossip to indulge in.

His lips twitched. "Why not Miss Darby? She is amiable and elegant, and would never dare use the word 'devil' in the presence of a man. She finds me more than barely tolerable, and doesn't attempt to insult me once every sixty seconds." He tipped his head to the side with a smirk, as if daring Grace to challenge him.

She never could resist a challenge.

"But—certainly there are other women you might choose that are not so …"

He raised his eyebrows.

"Irksome."

He gave an accusatory laugh. "You only find her irksome because I am now pursuing her. You are envious."

*How right you are.*

She scoffed, shifting so she faced him more fully. "That may be your wish, but I am not."

"Say what you will, but I can see it in your eyes."

"What exactly can you see?"

A breeze traveled past them as a cloud passed over the sun, rustling his hair and casting his face in shadow. Just like the cloud passing over the sun, a wicked grin passed over Lord Ramsbury's lips. "You love me."

Grace laughed, making her objection clear. "I love you?"

"You just said it."

"No! I do not love you."

"But you will."

"I will not. One cannot leap from hatred to love within a matter of days."

"Unless one possesses my skill." He winked.

Grace had never met a more shameless flirt in her life. What sort of charade had he been putting on for Miss Darby? Had he been pretending to fancy her as well? Grace gave him her sharpest glare, shaking her head in clear abhorrence.

The sound of his chuckling continued, and his blue eyes flashed with amusement. "If you knew how much I enjoyed the sight of that scowl you would not do it so often."

She bit her lip, raising one eyebrow. "Are you suggesting that I smile at you more?"

His eyes settled on her face in silence for a long moment. Grace had never seen such warmth in his gaze, mingled with a rare hesitation to speak. "Your smiles are every bit as enchanting as your scowls, Miss Grace. You are beautiful with any expression. Try as you might, but you have no way to escape my affections."

Why she allowed that blasted man to affect her, she couldn't understand or control. Her heart hammered in her chest, even as her mind told her to disregard his words and the warmth in his gaze. If Lord Ramsbury lost his inheritance, she decided he should seek employment in the London theater. He was a very skilled actor. An actor was all he was, and she was a spectator, enjoying a performance that would eventually end, foolish enough to believe for the briefest moment that it had been real.

"If Miss Darby knew you said that, I expect she would not be pleased," Grace said, a hint of bitterness sneaking into her voice.

He gave a soft smile. "I was teasing."

She frowned. "I do have a way to escape your affections? Please do tell me so I may take advantage."

"No, that you do not." He winked, picking up a new blade of grass to twirl between his fingers. "But I was teasing about Miss Darby. I have not begun a pursuit of her. And I never intend to. I only wished to see your reaction."

Relief crashed over Grace like a wave of the Brighton waters, but it was quickly followed by the sharp reminder of her role in his game. "If you think I was envious, you are wrong. I simply didn't think Miss Darby was the correct choice for you."

"Who would you consider the correct choice?"

She stumbled for a reply. "I'm not certain. But not Miss Darby. I am a skilled matchmaker, you know. Perhaps in time I can find you an alternative match, one much more compatible with you."

"You are a skilled matchmaker?" He made no effort to hide his surprise—or amusement.

"Why does that surprise you?"

He shrugged. "You do not strike me as a romantic."

"Of course, I am. Why do you suppose I have been reading *A Match of Great Consequence* at my leisure? Well, not any longer since my mother confiscated it from me." Grace sighed. Why was she telling Lord Ramsbury all of this? Why was she sitting on the grass having a conversation with him as if they were friends? It all seemed very wrong. There was also the fact that they were alone and unchaperoned, which would not bode well for her if they were seen.

Lord Ramsbury reached inside his jacket, a grin lighting his face as he withdrew a small book of his own. He turned the cover toward her, the words faintly visible among the worn leather.

"Where did you find that?" she half-whispered, afraid her mother might find a way to overhear from her place inside the house.

"I believe you mean to say 'where the *devil* did you find that.'"

She laughed with disbelief. He held the book up to the sunlight, a copy of the very book her mother had just stolen from her hands. *A Match of Great Consequence.* She had just told him the day before that she would be reading it today.

He smiled at her, a look so genuinely happy that for the briefest moment, she paused to admire him. He set the book down on the quilt and removed his jacket, draping it lazily on the quilt beside him. "I found it at the circulating library this morning with the intention to read with you," he said, pulling on his cravat to loosen it slightly. "I didn't think I would find you with a mathematics volume instead."

"I only chose the mathematics volume because..." she stopped herself, looking away from his expectant expression. She was not about to tell him she had been too distracted to read what she really wanted to read, all because of him and his charming smiles and their refusal to leave her mind. "Because I knew my mother would disapprove. If she had her way, I would be sitting indoors away from the sunlight, practicing my needlepoint and pianoforte and French, staying far away from my imagination."

He sprawled onto his back, propping his hand behind his head as he looked up at the clouds. "But instead you are out of doors practicing your insults on the next Earl of Coventry, with whom you are fraternizing *alone*, who is also a secret smuggler who brought you a second copy of that dreaded book."

Grace couldn't help but smile. "Precisely. I am the daughter every mother desires."

"I would not venture to say that." He turned his head toward her, and she had to stop herself from staring at the muscle in his arm that bent near his head, more visible now without his jacket. "But I would venture to say you are the woman every man desires."

She turned her gaze heavenward, shaking her head. Would he ever stop? "We must agree upon something right now, if you wish to remain tolerable."

Half his mouth lifted at the corner. "And what is that?"

"No flirting."

He laughed, as if her request were nothing short of ridiculous.

And impossible.

He sat up, fixing her with an intent gaze. "Not even once we are married?"

"Stop that!" She wished she could slap the broadening

smile off his face. Or kiss it. The contradiction both frustrated and confused her.

He released a heavy sigh of regret. "I cannot make a promise of it, but for your sake I will try."

"Good."

"But I do have a request to make of you in exchange."

She eyed him with misgiving. "Yes?"

"That after today you consider me a friend. Nothing less. I do enjoy spending time with you, Grace."

Her heart flipped at his casual use of her name, mingled with the intensity of his gaze. "But we mustn't do away with the formalities of miss and lord."

He grinned from his place on the ground, looking far too comfortable and at ease, while she felt her growing attraction to him unsettling to say the least. "I cannot think of you as *Miss* Grace any longer. Not after you have spoken so freely with me." He shook his head ever so slightly. "*Devil.*"

Grace resisted the urge to laugh again, proud of herself for remaining so composed. "Very well. A friend. But nothing more either."

"If you insist." He grinned up at her as she stood, brushing grass from her skirts.

She watched him carefully. Why was he still smiling? She had once again declared her disinterest in marrying him.

With quick steps she approached him, bending down to snatch his copy of *A Match of Great Consequence,* turning her back to him. "I hope you do not care if I borrow this."

"Where are you going?" he asked in an exasperated voice.

"Inside. If my mother saw us alone, she would ensure

that our friendship quickly became its own 'match of great consequence.'"

He chuckled. "But when may I see you again?"

She turned halfway toward him, one eyebrow raised. "I suspect you will find a way without my assistance."

"You are right. But I must see you as soon as possible, for I will need your assistance with a different matter. I need your help finding me a new match."

Grace's stomach twisted. Nothing sounded worse than watching Lord Ramsbury win the heart of an unassuming woman without any effort at all. It could happen easily—he did not need her assistance.

Her chest tightened with jealousy and regret, and she hated herself for it. Lord Ramsbury had fooled her again. He had made her feel special for a short while, entertaining himself with her, gaining a firm grip on her heart. Perhaps his intentions to marry her were real, but she couldn't believe he would ever love her, and she was in great danger of falling in love with him.

Without realizing it, she allowed her concerns to slip into her facial expression, her brows drawing together. She quickly corrected it. But not before Lord Ramsbury noticed.

"You are allowed to volunteer yourself as my match," he said in a reassuring voice.

She threw him a look of dismay that made him laugh. "Good day, my *lord*. She turned toward the house, eager to escape and realign her strange emotions.

"Good day, Grace," he called.

She gave him one final glance over her shoulder, squinting against the sun. He didn't seem intent to move from his place under the tree. Where had Harriett gone? If she had taken any part in Lord Ramsbury's appearance on their property then she would have a thorough explanation to make.

Grace walked past the gardens and through the door, stopping when she found her sister, leaned against the windowsill with a mischievous smile.

"Harriett!" Grace said, her jaw dropping. "Were you watching that entire time?"

"Yes." Her voice was giddy as she turned away from the window. "Oh, Grace, why can you not see how well suited you are?"

"You sound very much like me. Are you feeling well?"

Harriett groaned. "How can you say you do not like him? It is all right if you do."

"I do," Grace said in a quiet voice as she moved in front of the window, making no attempt to hide the truth. She gave a soft smile as she watched him take the mathematics book into his lap, flipping through the pages. "And that is the problem."

"Why is that a problem?"

"Because he is only pretending." Grace gave her sister a rueful glance, pretending that it didn't hurt as much as it did.

"You do not know that for certain."

Harriett was right—it wasn't certain. But it was probable. And Grace didn't dare risk her heart for a slight chance. Pretending to despise him was much safer. "I will need to know for certain that he is genuine. Until then, I cannot allow myself to feel anything for him. I made that mistake before. At any rate, I don't think he will propose again. He asked me to assist him in finding a new woman for him to pursue."

"You cannot be serious."

"I am." Grace handed her sister the rose she had taken from the gardens. The disappointment in Harriett's eyes matched the feeling in Grace's heart, biting and stabbing, creating permanent marks. Grace couldn't begin to understand the array of things she felt—jealousy, anger, fear… elation, delight, amusement, all tied to one man. How was it possible to feel so much at once? How could one person inspire so much inner turmoil?

"Are you going to help him find a new match?" Harriett asked.

"I don't see a reason not to."

Harriett raised her eyebrows. "Because you want him for yourself?"

"I do not." Even Grace heard the rising pitch to her own voice—evidence of a lie.

She scowled out the window as Harriett laughed. Lord Ramsbury stood, leaving the book behind on the quilt, stretching his back.. He draped his jacket over his arm, glancing back at the house as he walked away.

With a shriek, Grace ducked below the window before he could see her spying. Harriett crouched down beside her, fresh giggles racking her petite frame. "You do."

Letting out a long sigh, Grace didn't even bother denying it.

"Perhaps some distance from Lord Ramsbury will help to clarify your thoughts," Harriet said. "Would you accompany me to the shops of town? If you are to take all of my pin money for the next several months I would like to have a hand in what you purchase with it."

"Oh, Harriett. Mama and Papa spoke to me today. Their debts are extensive, and they urged me to take the prospect of marriage more seriously. I suspect they will speak to you of it soon as well. They feel they cannot sustain us much longer. Our pin money could very well be gone."

Harriett's face twisted in shock. "Is the situation truly so dire?"

"I'm afraid so. They seemed quite anxious over the matter, especially Mama. They said we might have to remove to a smaller home outside of Brighton. I hope you will consider William more seriously."

"If the matter is so urgent, then what is keeping you from accepting Lord Ramsbury?"

Grace sighed. "I will not sacrifice being loved for anything. A loveless marriage would be worse than a life of poverty."

Harriett grimaced. "You would not even sacrifice it for limitless hats and gowns and slippers?"

"No."

The skin between Harriett's eyebrows pinched. "I suppose I wouldn't either. But to have both would be ideal." Her face slowly lifted back into a smile, dispelling the anxiety that hovered in the air. "So… shall we visit the shops? Even if we cannot purchase anything, it would be a welcome diversion."

Grace sighed. The shops did not brighten her mood the way they did Harriett's. But they would indeed be a welcome distraction. She could only hope distance from Lord Ramsbury would give her thoughts and heart the clarity she sought.

# Chapter 10

"I believe another proposal is in order," Edward said as he walked through the entry hall of Clemsworth. He had caught Henry on his way out of the house, eager to discuss his progress concerning Grace.

Edward had seen the envy in her eyes when he had spoken of other women. He had leapt from barely tolerable to a friend in just one day. By the end of the week he would take the leap to potential husband without any problem at all.

"Do you really think she will give you the answer you hope for?" Henry's voice was filled with doubt.

"Well—no." Edward rubbed his jaw. Even if she was developing feelings for him, she was still far too stubborn. "I may need more time. Yes. I will find a way to see her tomorrow. She still acts as if my very presence is insulting." He laughed. "And she has a complete inability to hide a single thing she wishes to say. She enjoys reading more than anything else, and I found the book she has been reading at the circulating library and brought it to her. She stole it from my hands as if it belonged to her, and then marched away from me." His face had sprung into a full smile as he relayed the morning to his brother, who had now fixed him with a look of amusement.

"You are falling in love with her."

Edward scoffed. "I am not."

Leaning against the banister, Henry raised one eyebrow. "You are. And what is wrong with that?"

Edward could think of many things wrong with that. Her rejections would begin to hurt. His game would not longer be only a game. If he lost his heart all over again, he would never recover. The ability to be in control of his emotions had been a battle his entire life. He couldn't lose now.

"I am not falling in love with her," Edward said, a firmness in his voice, as if he were trying to convince himself more than Henry.

"You denial means nothing, brother. I see it in your eyes."

"What do you know of love?" Edward snapped. "Have you ever felt it?"

Henry sighed, starting toward the door again. "I haven't. But if I do I will be wise enough to fight for it. I will not take it with a lazy hand, one that could be disarmed at any moment."

Edward watched as Henry gripped the door handle, turning to offer a final remark. A heaviness settled in his gaze. "But if you are determined to marry Miss Grace, you ought to hurry. Papa's health is declining rapidly. You might consider visiting his room. Mama must rest and Juliet refuses to leave his side."

Edward nodded, his jaw tightening. "I will go see him. How long would you determine he has to live?"

"A week, perhaps two. The physician said as much upon his last visit."

A fold of anxiety blossomed in Edward's chest as Henry left the house.

He made his way to his father's bedchamber, stopping in the doorway, concealed from view. His mother sat in a chair beside her husband. She leaned over the bed, her elbow pressed into the mattress with her head resting on her hand. Juliet sat beside her, a frown pinching her youthful face.

Edward's heart stung at the sight, and at the detachment he felt to his father. It filled him with more sorrow to see the pain in his mother's face than it did to know his father would soon die. He wished the relationship he had shared with his uncle had been the same with his father. But his father had always had a very gruff exterior, never softening for anything. Edward had seen the same desperation in Juliet's face that he had felt as a young boy, always waiting to be noticed and loved.

Walking into the room, Edward placed his hand on his mother's shoulder, startling her. "Sorry, Mama," he whispered. His father lay asleep, a paleness to his face that Edward had never seen. "You must go, rest, breathe fresh air. It is not well for you or Juliet to be here all hours of the day."

She rubbed her eyes, clutching his hand as she stood up.

"Edward," Juliet's clear voice cut the air. "Must I leave too?"

"Yes, I'm afraid I must insist. You need to go play, explore," he tapped her nose, "and smile."

Her large blue eyes settled on her father once again.

"I will be back soon, Papa," she said, though he couldn't possibly have heard her.

Edward stared down at his father, his lungs filling with apprehension. It had only been a matter of days since he had been in the room discussing his disinheritance, and already his father appeared much worse. His skin emitted a grayish hue, his breathing rapid and shallow as he slept. His illness had begun to consume all his organs, his very life and breath. A stab of grief hit Edward squarely in the chest. It surprised him.

Without warning, his father's eyes flew open, blinking as he surveyed his surroundings. His gaze found Edward, settling on his face with recognition.

"Why are you here?" he rasped.

"I thought I might spend a moment with my ailing father."

He grunted, rolling to one side as he searched for the handkerchief beside his pillow. He coughed into it, a wet, painful sound. He smacked his lips, drawing the reddened handkerchief away from his mouth. "You ought to be spending all your hours with that Miss Weston. Your mother told me much concerning her."

Edward hesitated. "What did she say?"

"She said Miss Grace seems the perfect match for you." His father's words were slurred.

Edward laughed, dropping his chin to his chest. "Miss Grace does not seem to agree, unfortunately. She refused my first proposal and does not seem inclined to ever accept me."

His father's gaze intensified, growing clearer and more aware. "Your mother also said you were becoming the man you used to be. Determined, indomitable, joyful, and a bit more intelligent in your decisions. If Miss Grace has played any part in this, you ought to leave my side and find her at once. You have little to lose in proposing a second time."

"The man I used to be?" Edward bristled. What could his father mean by that?

"Yes. Before my brother died. Before you lost yourself."

Edward's jaw clenched. If only his father knew the role he had played in that change. After his uncle had died Edward had become a young man without a father to guide him, lost in grief. He had found a place in society, earning a reputation as a shameless flirt, and later, after Miss Buxton's rejection, an indolent and careless gambler and drunk. His father had done nothing to help him. If he had reached out a hand even once, Edward might have stopped his downward plunge. He might have seen the light again.

Only when he had met Grace—the true Grace—had he again determined to find the true version of himself. He wanted to be a man like his uncle. Honorable, kind, selfless, determined. When he was with Grace he couldn't help but tease her, but he also couldn't help but strive harder to be a better man. Only a better man would ever deserve a woman like Grace Weston. He shook his mind of her intelligent brown eyes, smirking lips, and fierce eyebrows.

"Does that mean you wish to bestow my inheritance upon me once again, without stipulation?" Edward asked.

His father shook his head, his eyes rolling back as he coughed. "No," he said, the word strangled. "As I said before, you must be engaged before my death. Only then will I know you are in earnest. An earl is nothing without a countess. Your mother has been my life. Without her I would have been lost."

Edward still felt betrayed. All his father had ever given him was this inheritance, and even then, it had not been given by his father, but by Edward's birthright—by the laws of primogeniture. To find a way around the law through extensive effort, just to destroy his eldest son's livelihood was more nefarious than Edward ever thought his father could be.

He wished he had never told Grace of his father's stipulation. It led her to question everything he did and said.

"Continue to rest, Papa." Edward patted his father's leg through the blanket. "And I will continue to romance Miss Grace."

A whisper of a smile crossed his father's face before it dissolved in a frown. "If your success with her is unlikely, consider seeking a different woman. As you can see, my time here is short."

Edward's heart burned with grief again, just as he shook away his father's suggestion. No other woman would suffice now, not since Edward had spent more time with Grace. He was realizing that he didn't want a woman that would bend to his every request, ramble flattering nonsense in his ear, and giggle in the false manner Grace once had. She had played the role of the common Brighton woman quite well, but he was discovering that she was all but common. She was intriguing. Fascinating. And utterly maddening.

"Hope isn't yet lost," Edward said, standing. He gave his father a heartfelt look. "But I would appreciate if you would stay alive as long as possible."

"If the woman wants to marry you, she will do so whether you ask today or next week," his father grumbled. Edward smiled. His father's gruff honesty had never failed. But his father didn't know Grace. Even if she did have feelings for Edward, she would never marry him without persistent effort on his part. Her pride wouldn't allow it. Just as his pride wouldn't allow him to receive no for an answer.

But his heart was becoming more and more involved, swallowing his pride in small increments. Whether she married him or not would depend on whose determination was stronger. And Edward had never met a more determined lady than Grace.

"Stay alive, Papa. Juliet and Henry and Mama will miss you. As will I." He clamped his jaw, watching for any sign that his words had touched his father's semblance of emotions.

"Please look after Juliet," his father said in a barely audible voice. "She will need a man's influence, and I will not be here. I'm afraid I have never been present for my children. And for that I offer my… belated apology."

Edward couldn't believe what he had just heard. Pins prickled over his heart, drawing out old memories, sending them trickling down through his body—speaking to his father and being dismissed, greeting his father after a long journey, only to be given a brief glance. There was much Edward wanted to say, but to not accept a dying man's apology was cruel.

His shoulders tightened as he met his father's gaze. "I will look after Juliet the way Uncle looked after me."

A shadow passed over his father's face—a shadow of regret.

Edward gave him a soft smile as he left the room in silence, closing the door behind him. He breathed the fresh air of the vast hallway, clearing his lungs of the stuffiness in his father's chambers.

A familiar, quiet sobbing reached him from down the hall. He turned to the left to see Juliet, sitting against the wall with her knees pulled to her chest. Grief struck again, digging into Edward's heart like knives. His mother stood above Juliet, struggling to console her.

Edward walked closer, stopping above his sister. Her crying had seized her small frame, causing her shoulders to shake as tears fell down her cheeks.

His mother turned to him, her own eyes red. "She will not listen. I cannot leave her here, Edward." She looked on the brink of collapse, in desperate need of rest.

"I will stay with her." He placed his hand on his mother's cheek. "Not to worry." His mother hid her emotions well, just like his father. Being strong for the sake of another was exhausting her. She covered his hand with hers, gratitude shining in her eyes before she stepped away, rubbing her forehead as she walked down the long hall.

"Juliet," Edward said, stooping down. She lifted her face from where it was buried in her arm, blinking away her tears. "Papa requested that I ask a favor of you."

Juliet sniffed. "What is it?"

"He asked that you accompany me to town to purchase one of his favorite confections from the baker. I am told I cannot be trusted among so many fine treats, for I will return home with the lot of them."

One side of her mouth twitched. "Why did he not send a servant?"

"Because he knows that only you can select the best Shrewsbury cake, and that I will likely eat it on my travel back if you are not present to stop me."

She giggled, swatting at her cheeks to rid them of the tears. "But Papa does not feel well enough to eat a Shrewsbury cake."

"Then perhaps, with a bit of luck, he will give it to you." Edward winked.

Her eyes brightened before her face melted into contemplation. "We might purchase multiple… perchance Papa *does* want his."

Edward laughed, extending his hand to help her up from the floor. She dusted off her skirts, gleaming with excitement. Her face was still splotched from her tears, but the joy in her eyes outshone it.

"Off to the bakery we go," he said.

Juliet smiled, and the sight warmed Edward to his core. To know he had been responsible for that smile felt like his life's greatest accomplishment. Today he would concentrate on his sister, on bringing her comfort amid her worry and fear, instead of focusing on his own. He could wait until the next day to worry himself with Grace. Distance from her would be beneficial, and would give him the strength of mind to scold his heart into indifference.

It would also give him time to plan his next proposal.

# Chapter 11

Harriett stopped at the window of the cordwainer shop, admiring a pair of boots in the window. Grace had been concealing her boredom for the last hour, her mind focused on everything but the leather boots. They had already stopped at the millinery, and the milliner had greeted Harriett as if she were an old friend, not merely a customer. After both Grace and Harriett had been matched to a set of colored ribbons best suited to their complexions and eyes, Harriett had discussed her next headpiece in great detail, and how it would match her favorite dress.

Grace's stomach rumbled as she stared at the confectioner's shop across the cobbled streets. She had not yet eaten that day, and she had a definite weakness for Brighton's Shrewsbury cakes. The Brighton baker made the best she had ever tasted, and the scant coins in her reticule jingled with temptation.

"Harriett," Grace said, pulling her sister's own tempted gaze from the cordwainer shop window. "If you accompany me to the bakery I will purchase you a treat of your choice."

"But the boots…"

"… are far too expensive for your current state."

Harriett released a sigh of deep regret. "I know. It is a dreadful shame."

"Indeed," Grace said, her voice airy as she stared at the sweets shop. If she could eat a Shrewsbury cake then the trip to town would be worth every moment. Linking her arm through Harriett's to prevent her escape, Grace waited for a gig to pass before crossing the road. Just the thought of the flaky, lemony biscuit made her mouth water.

Reaching the door, she stepped aside as a man exited the shop, nearly colliding with her.

"Pardon me," she said, glancing up to see a set of familiar and handsome blue eyes. She stepped back, her heart thrashing around like a wild thing in her chest. Lord Ramsbury appeared just as surprised to see her standing in the doorway of the shop as she had been to see him. Why was it that after years of only seeing him around town occasionally, she now seemed to find him everywhere she turned? His ever-present smile had been wiped from his face by her abrupt appearance, but he soon recovered, lifting his mouth into a devastating grin.

"Are you following me? I am flattered that you could not resist my company for more than an hour, but don't you think the public will start to wonder if there is an agreement between us?"

Grace willed her heart to slow. "You would like the public to think that. You would like that very much."

"I cannot deny it."

Before she could stop it, a silly grin had plastered itself over her face. She pressed it down as quickly as she could manage, clearing her throat as she looked down at little Juliet, who clung to her brother's arm. Her eyes were rimmed in red, as if she had recently been crying.

"What brings you to the bakery?" Grace asked the girl with a smile.

Juliet glanced up at her brother, as if unsure of whether she was allowed to speak. With a shy grin, she said, "We wanted to get a Shrewsbury cake for my papa. I was meant stop Edward from purchasing too many, but he did so anyway." She giggled, a soft, musical sound.

Grace glanced up at Lord Ramsbury, her heart skipping all over again at his loving smile as he stared down at his sister. Grace cursed herself for caring. She had spent three years creating a monstrous image of Lord Ramsbury in her mind. To see him now, not at all how she had imagined, was thoroughly unsettling. His eyes found hers, remnants of his loving smile still shining through them. "I cannot resist Shrewsbury cakes," he said with a shrug.

Harriett gripped Grace's arm, recalling her attention. She lowered her voice in her ear, a mischievous smile lurking behind her words. "I will return to the cordwainer shop so you may be alone. I saw Miss Daventry enter. I shall walk home with her."

Grace almost protested, but caught Lord Ramsbury watching. Harriett offered him a polite nod before hurrying away.

"She has set her fancy on a pair of boots," Grace explained, attempting to excuse her sister's abrupt departure. "She could not bear to be apart from them for the smallest moment."

"Just as you could not bear to be apart from me," Lord Ramsbury said, a teasing glint in his eyes.

Grace chose to ignore his comment, as well as the flutter it caused in the pit of her stomach. "I hope you left a cake for me." Grace rose on the balls of her feet, straining her neck to see around him into the shop. "That is why I am here."

"We took them all," Juliet said.

Grace's eyes widened. "All of them?"

"Edward is quite hungry."

Grace noticed the large box Lord Ramsbury was using to hold the door open. An older couple was waiting to exit the shop, their passage blocked by him. Stepping aside, Lord Ramsbury came to a stop beside Grace on the busy street, the warm scents of the bakery drifting away as the door closed.

"Juliet had the responsibility of stopping me from purchasing all of them." Lord Ramsbury opened the box to peer inside. "But she encouraged me instead." He gave his sister a teasing frown. "So the fault is yours, not mine."

Juliet giggled.

He turned to Grace. "But you are in luck. I am a very generous man, and so I will offer you as many Shrewsbury cakes as you would like."

She narrowed her eyes with suspicion. "And what do you require in return?"

He chuckled. "Why do you assume I require compensation?"

"Well, if you truly love Shrewsbury cakes as much as I do, then I know you would not sacrifice one, and certainly not multiple, unless it was for a very beneficial purpose."

He exchanged a glance with Juliet before casting Grace a winning smile. "You are right. I should ask for something in exchange."

"No, I—" Grace clamped her mouth shut. Why had she given him the blasted idea?

"I would request that you spend the afternoon with Juliet and me. We are quite bored with one another's company, you see."

Juliet stomped on his boot, throwing him a frown that only seemed half-genuine. "How dare you say you are tired of me? I'm telling Mama."

Edward pinched her nose, and she swatted his hand away with a laugh. "You know I could never tire of you, Juliet."

She smirked. "I know."

Grace watched the exchange with a smile, letting out a quiet sigh of misgiving. She had hoped to spend the day far away from Lord Ramsbury. It seemed that every time she saw him, his effect on her grew stronger. He haunted her thoughts, and he did strange things to her heart and the rhythm of her breathing. But a small part of her—a weak part—wanted to be near him. And a large part of her wanted a Shrewsbury cake.

"Very well," she said. "Harriett is with her friend, Miss Daventry, so I will spend the afternoon with you. I do enjoy *Juliet's* company." She smiled down at the young girl, trying to ignore the deep laugh of amusement coming from Lord Ramsbury.

Juliet's large blue eyes stared up at Grace, a deep affection glowing there that surprised her. Juliet snatched Grace's hand, pulling her toward the mantua maker's shop. "Would you like to see the dress that I wish to wear for my first ball?" Juliet asked.

Grace nodded, her own grin increasing. The young girl's excitement was infectious and refreshing. They started toward the shop, with Lord Ramsbury trailing behind them. Grace spoke to Juliet about all the styles of gowns she preferred, as well as her favorite colors and trims. Grace did not know nearly as much as Harriett did about gowns, but she was able to keep Juliet entertained with her stories of the gowns she had worn.

"My very first ball occurred when I was sixteen years old." From the corner of her eye, Grace could see Lord Ramsbury behind them, listening intently. "The ball was held during summer at the residence of the Livingston family. I wore a yellow dress with a blue sash at the waist. It had embroidered vines across the bodice, and added lace on the sleeves. It is still the most beautiful gown I have ever worn."

Juliet's eyes shone with awe. "Did you dance with many gentlemen?"

Grace's spine prickled as Lord Ramsbury stepped up beside her. "She danced with me."

"Truly?" Juliet gave a tiny gasp.

"Yes."

Grace stared at the ground ahead, focusing her gaze on one cobblestone that stood higher than the rest, loose from constant feet trampling over it. Her heart squeezed with the memory of that ball, of the hope that had burned in her heart, the feeling that she was special. A man of consequence had chosen her to dance with all evening. He had set his attention on her, and all her friends had declared that he would be intent to further their acquaintance. Her heart had soared with excitement and joy and romance. She had felt very much like a character from her favorite books. Important, wanted, beautiful.

And then came the memory of her second ball, four months later. She still remembered the effort she had taken in front of the looking glass, Harriett at her side. They had debated for twenty minutes over one curl, whether it should hang around her face or be pinned atop her head. The decision had been made to pin it away from her face. Her stomach had fluttered with fear and anticipation as she entered the ballroom. Her cheeks had flushed as she saw Lord Ramsbury. She had approached him, waiting for him to acknowledge her, but he never did. His eyes had met hers only once before drifting away.

She had watched him from the corner of the room for most of the night, tears burning behind her eyes as her friends questioned why she was not with him. But he had found a different lady, and then another, and another to dance with. And Grace had remained alone the entire evening, too dejected to dance at all.

After that night, Grace had set her heart against Lord Ramsbury, determining that the man could not be trusted. His words, his promises, his flattery were all false.

*False.* His attention toward her now… how could it be anything but?

"Is it true, Miss Grace?" Juliet's small voice cut through her thoughts. "Or is my brother jesting again?"

Grace swallowed. "No, it is true."

"Did she look beautiful in her yellow dress, Edward?"

Grace waited for a string of insincere words to flow from his mouth, to hear all the things she knew to be a lie.

He was silent for a long moment. "I wish I remembered," he said finally. "But it was very long ago. I was a fool to have forgotten so quickly. If I had known her then as I know her now, I would have kept her close and never let her escape, no matter how much she wanted to. But I would wager, as one only could, that Miss Grace looked beautiful in that yellow dress."

Grace's heart pounded in her ears as she looked up at him. Regret loomed in his eyes, mingled with an unspoken apology.

"That is the dress!" Juliet's exclamation made Grace jump. She looked at the window ahead, an extravagant pink gown hanging on the display.

"You will look stunning in that, Juliet," Grace said, keeping the tremor from her voice. "Only a few more years and you may wear one just like it."

Juliet ran up for a closer look, practically pressing her nose against the glass.

Lord Ramsbury turned toward Grace, speaking in hushed tones. "Our father's condition has been very upsetting for her. I am so glad we found you here. I could never speak with her so knowledgeably about dresses, a subject which never fails to make her smile. I must thank you for that."

Grace smiled, relieved that Lord Ramsbury had changed the subject. "Harriett has given me all the practice I need in discussing fashion." She looked up at him, his gaze still fixed on Juliet.

A sadness settled over his brow. "It will be difficult for her to wear black for so long. And even more difficult to be without her father."

Grace thought of her own father, similarly detached and distant. She had grown up desperate for his attention, but it had never come. He spent his days shut away in his study. Rarely did he speak more than a brief sentence to her, unless it involved a topic of seriousness. Uncle Cornelius had always felt like more of a father, treating her with love and kindness.

Grace had eventually given up trying to win her own father's attention, filling the emptiness within her with stories and dreams of one day marrying a man that would be a kind and loving father to their children.

Lord Ramsbury sighed. "She loves our father, despite his avoidance of her for most of her life. I do not understand." His brow contracted into a serious expression, one Grace was still unaccustomed to seeing.

"Something must fill the empty spaces within us," Grace said, fixing her eyes on Juliet. "Her father left emptiness within her, and so she has filled it herself. Some allow it to fill with anger, or resentment, or sorrow, but she has filled it with love of her own—the very thing she felt was missing. You can never go wrong filling emptiness and abandonment with love. It strengthens and builds, while other things only destroy." Grace felt Lord Ramsbury's gaze on her, and she met his eyes. "What did you fill yours with?"

He looked down at the ground, sliding his boot over the road. "Nothing I am proud of."

"It is never too late to change."

He breathed deeply through his nose, crossing his arms as if to keep himself from breaking. "First was my father's distant nature, then my uncle's death. I lost sight of all motivation to be good and honorable. I did not treat others as I should have, and I am very sorry you were made to endure that."

She looked down, twisting her hands together.

"And then…" he paused. "Then I was persuaded to believe I could be loved by a woman that I cared for deeply, only to be deceived. I felt my heart could not tolerate another blow. I filled myself with anger and self-pity." He shook his head. "I never want to be that man again."

Grace stared at him, shocked at how wrong her assumptions had been. He had been hurt. His circumstances and misfortunes had sculpted many of his decisions. There was more depth to him than she had ever thought possible. The devil-may-care, debonair, rakish image that she had connected with his name was not completely true. It was another act. A way for him to cope with his losses with assumed dignity.

"Do you still think of her often?" Grace asked, afraid of the answer. "The woman that broke your heart?"

He turned his gaze down to Grace, causing her skin to tingle and her heart to skitter. The blue of his eyes seemed brighter here, magnified by the sunlight around them. "No. She was not the right match for me."

"No?"

The faintest smile touched his lips. "No."

Grace felt her own lips curving as she stared into his eyes, a cursed blush tingling on her cheeks. Her entire body flooded with warmth, spiraling up from her toes, spreading through her chest. But shards of ice, brought to life by recent memories of her first ball, stole her smile and the reassurances of her heart. Lord Ramsbury claimed to be different, but what if it was all a lie?

A large stagecoach passed on the road, the jarring sound enough to clear her mind.

"And so I am reminded," Grace's posture straightened, her smile disappearing. "You asked that I find a match for you, and I have. Miss Rose Daventry, my sister's friend. She is a lovely and accomplished young lady. Unlike me, she truly does possess talent on the pianoforte and is fluent in French, and she doesn't care for reading nonsense. She is very well connected and has a wonderful family. She is with my sister at this very moment if you wish to meet her." As the words escaped her, Grace felt a gnawing emptiness, and not just her hungry stomach.

Lord Ramsbury studied her face, as if he were trying to decipher something important. She looked down, uncomfortable with his attention. He was probably thinking of how pleased he was with Grace for finding him such a talented and sensible woman. Why did it matter? Grace had already decided that she would never marry him, not if it meant she was only an apparatus for keeping his title.

Grace had often heard Miss Daventry speak of her desire to make a well-established match, not caring whether love had any involvement and Lord Ramsbury only needed a marriage to keep his inheritance. Aside from wealth and possessions, Miss Daventry had also stated that she preferred a handsome man, though she did not require it. Lord Ramsbury was surely that. How much more perfect could it be? The dread that settled in her stomach belied her sentiments.

"Will you meet her?" Grace asked, hoping her voice would break the trance he seemed to be under as he examined her face.

Lord Ramsbury's lips closed, creating a soft smile that made her heart flip. "I don't wish to meet her at all."

"Why not? She is very amiable, and any person who has made her acquaintance will endorse her character. She is well-mannered and polite, and is also—"

He stopped her with a touch to her forearm, making her words stand still. Her skin burned under his touch. "I do not want you to find me a match."

Grace lifted her chin, her defenses rising with new strength. "Why?"

"I was only teasing when I asked you."

"But it is no trouble, truly. I will introduce you to Miss Daventry." She nodded quickly. "We may find her this very moment."

He let out a sigh of frustration, turning to face her more fully. Juliet had turned away from the window, watching their exchange with piqued interest. He opened his mouth to speak.

"Juliet is eager to rejoin us, my lord," Grace stammered, stopping the words he was about to say.

He glanced over his shoulder at his sister before looking down at Grace again. She pressed her lips together, staring at his cravat rather than his eyes, a much safer alternative.

"Edward," he muttered. "Please call me Edward."

Grace steadied her breathing. "I cannot use your Christian name."

"We are friends, are we not?"

Grace would have agreed, but she knew it was not normal to have a fervent desire to kiss a mere *friend*. To wrap her arms around his neck and feel his around her, holding her close, promising he would never forget her—that he would always love her—and having those promises proven somehow. But doubt still lingered in her mind, etched there like engravings on wood.

She raised her eyes to his face, settling on the smile on his lips, the belonging in his eyes. Even if none of it was real, she was too weak to desert it today.

"I suppose," she said. "At any rate, you did already use *my* Christian name."

"I could not help myself." He chuckled.

Juliet approached with slow steps, as if she were afraid of interrupting an important conversation. Grace wondered what the passersby might be thinking of their position, standing so near to one another with so many quiet words and smiles passing between them. Every moment she spent with him was a risk to her reputation, unless she intended to accept his proposal. Which she didn't.

Did she?

# Chapter 12

"May we look for shells on the beach?" Juliet asked as she approached them. "We may eat our Shrewsbury cakes there too. Do you suppose the birds will come if we leave pieces in the sand for them?"

Grace stepped away from Edward, bending close to Juliet's height. "Surely the birds do not like Shrewsbury cakes."

"How could they not?" Juliet scowled.

"She is simply scheming to have more cakes for herself," Edward said, his eyes narrowed in accusation.

Juliet's features flashed with understanding, and a giggle escaped her. Grace laughed, easily infected by Juliet's joy. She admired the young girl's strength. It was a rare talent to smile amid adversity, and Juliet was very skilled at it.

The trio walked through the market on their way to the nearest side of the beach. It did not take long to reach the ocean from any point in Brighton. They passed an array of strangers, tourists passing through the town that the Prince Regent made so alluring. People that came from outside of Brighton expected to find a town filled with the lavish lifestyles of the prince, but what they found was simply a town flooded with people, and wrought with many strange traditions.

One of the greatest attractions to Brighton was the waters that were rumored to remedy all ailments. One entered the water in a wooden bathing machine, pulled out with ropes by one of the hired 'dippers.' They would then be lowered into the sea, and the precious water was expected to draw out impurities and pain. Grace knew it to be false, but there were some that vowed the waters had healed them.

Grace loved the idea of such a fantastical thing, whether she believed it or not. In her imagination she dreamt that the waters held more than a cure. She wished that they held the answers she sought. Was Edward genuine? Or was he simply a ruse? Just like the waters meant to draw people in, only to be disappointed, Grace feared he was drawing her to him, only to break her heart.

Her thoughts remained distant on their walk to the ocean, though she continued to make light conversation with Juliet, who clung to her hand.

They reached the end of the beach nearest to Clemsworth, the place where Grace had seen Lord Ramsbury taunting his sister.

Grace began scavenging for shells among the damp sand, following the lead of Juliet. Seagrass grew in patches around them, waving with the gentle breeze. Juliet crouched close to the water, digging her fingers into the sand.

Edward approached from behind, smiling down at

Grace as she searched the ground for shells. She kept her ankles covered, lifting her skirts just enough to avoid getting them soiled. Her hair was coming slowly untethered by the winds as they picked up speed, stirring the ocean up in multi-blue toned peaks. She laughed as Juliet held up a misshapen shell, a gnarled brown one covered in white streaks.

Edward still watched her, his grin growing larger. Her curiosity couldn't be contained. "What are you staring at?" She squinted against the sun, pushing back a pesky strand of hair that fell on her forehead.

"Nothing." Edward made an attempt to press down his grin, but it resurfaced.

She straightened her posture, tossing aside the small conical shell she had just collected. "I have become well acquainted with that smile of yours. I know what it means."

"Now I am curious. What do you think it means?"

"It means you are amused. Am I correct?"

He laughed. "Partially."

She pushed back a chunk of dark hair that had blown in her eyes. "And what am I missing?"

He stepped over the shell she had dropped, his closeness catching her by surprise. He touched her cheek, tucking a strand of hair behind her ear. The warmth of his fingers matched the warmth in his eyes, a blue that matched the ocean behind him.

"You are missing a very important detail. It means I find you amusing, yes, but it also means I find you enchanting."

Her heart leapt in her chest, and her cheeks flooded with heat. She stepped away, swallowing hard. "I thought we agreed that you were not allowed to flirt."

He chuckled. "Once again, I'm afraid, I could not help myself. You are begging to be flirted with." He touched her face again, sending a string of tingles over her neck. "And the color of your cheeks signify that my efforts are not in vain." The teasing in his voice stung deep in Grace's chest, reminding her that this was merely a game.

"Please. I want to hear no more of it. We reached an agreement."

"I promise I will not flirt with any other woman as long as I live. Only you." His hair had become mussed with the wind, falling over his forehead.

The teasing note still hung in his voice. She couldn't trust that he would only flirt with her. He found far too much pleasure in being a shameless flirt.

Grace took a step backward, creating a much-needed distance between them. He chuckled, apparently still amused by her efforts to avoid him. She crossed the beach, pretending to search for shells among the sand. Edward followed close behind her, making her palms sweat and her legs shake.

She was close—too close to surrendering. Without a doubt he intended to push the subject further, so she turned around with her hands planted on her hips, prepared to offer a diatribe that would erase the smile on his face.

When she faced him, however, he extended his hand, three small shells in his palm. She scowled in confusion.

"We must not be distracted," he said with urgency. "Juliet has already gathered at least ten shells and she simply cannot win."

Juliet's head whipped in his direction. She giggled, his challenge leading her to scour the sand faster. Grace turned her gaze back to Edward, who gave her a soft smile before bending down to dig through the sand.

Taking a moment to gather herself, Grace joined the hunt, laughing as she placed shell after shell in her hands until she could hold no more. A large shell protruded from the sand near a rock, shining like a piece of buried treasure. Edward spotted it at the same moment Grace did, racing across the sand to claim it. She was closer, and managed to snatch it up before he reached it.

"Ha!" she said, clamping it between her hands. "The largest shell is mine."

"I did see it first."

"You did not!"

Edward laughed, tossing his handful of shells on the sand beside him. He rolled up the sleeves of his white shirt. "Give it to me."

Grace hurried across the sand, moving away from him. *What the devil did he plan to do?*

"Steal it from her, Edward!" Juliet called with a giggle. Grace gasped. She was beginning to question her original positive opinion of the girl.

"You will do no such thing." Grace lifted a finger, warning him with a look.

The grin on his face resembled the one she had seen him give Juliet when his hands had been filled with wet sand. Now his hands were empty, prepared to wrestle a meaningless shell from her.

He took two more steps toward her, and Grace's resolve fled. With a shriek, she flung the shell across the beach. It landed in front of Juliet, who scooped it up with a look of triumph. Edward burst into laughter, his shoulders shaking. Grace laughed too, covering one half of her face with her palm. By the time her laughter subsided, her stomach ached.

"You are a wicked man." Grace scowled, the effort half-hearted.

He sighed, a grin still pulling at his mouth. "And so the insults return."

"I am sorry, but you are begging to be insulted." Throwing him an apologetic look, she bit her lower lip.

His eyes settled on her mouth. "And you are begging to be kissed."

Her heart thumped so hard she was afraid he could hear it. She had the urge to run again, just as she had when he had tried to steal the shell. To share a kiss here beside the ocean would be more romantic than anything she had ever read in a book. It would also be more dangerous. Smugglers and spies and highwaymen robberies could not compare to the harm a kiss from Lord Ramsbury would inflict. But he was there, close enough to touch, to smell, to feel. Her skin burned with longing, but self discipline had always been one of her strongest virtues.

"And so the flirting returns," Grace said, her voice more weak than she intended. Stepping away from him took great effort, but she did it. She expected to feel strong, but the distance between them only made her feel weaker.

Juliet sat on the sand counting her shells. How improper it would have been to kiss Edward with her so near. How improper it would have been to kiss him at all, especially out in the open air where they could easily be seen. She scolded herself for even entertaining the thought. The ocean breeze helped to cool her cheeks enough to face Edward again. "I must return home."

He drew a deep breath. "We will walk with you."

"No, I would prefer to walk alone."

His eyes roamed her face. "If you are certain."

"I am." She threw him a smile, but the burning within her made it difficult. "Good day," she said, turning around.

She only made it two steps before she heard his voice again.

"Wait."

Her feet stopped but she didn't turn around. Her heart pounded as she listened to his footsteps on the sand behind her. He touched her elbow.

She prepared a list of excuses in her mind, reasons she could not stay any longer before turning to face him.

"You cannot leave without this."

She looked down at his hand, where he held a thick Shrewsbury cake, half wrapped in brown paper, flecked with lemon shavings and dried berries. Even in the open air, the sweet scent wafted up to her nostrils, filling her with warmth.

She smiled, taking the cake from his hand. "You did say I could have *multiple*."

He laughed, shaking his head in amusement as he returned to the box on the sand, withdrawing two more. She pressed her lips together expectantly as he wrapped them up and handed them over.

"Thank you," she said in a resolute voice, lifting her pile of cakes to her nose to inhale the warm aroma.

He tipped his head down as he laughed. "You are quite welcome." He glanced at her from under his lashes, a look she was sure had served to steal many hearts without assistance. "It is the only reason you came, after all. Is it not?"

She was sure he wanted her to deny it, so it came naturally to give him the opposite. "You are right. For what other reason would I willingly spend the afternoon with you?" She hoped her smile would soften her words as she walked away.

His laugh followed her all the way to the edge of the beach, where she stepped onto the cobblestones. She savored the sound, inviting a stirring into her heart, a radiating warmth that would not leave her as she walked toward home. She told herself over and over as she walked, that his every word and action were false, but it did little to stop the feelings within her. Two words challenged it all. *What if.*

What if Edward really did care for her?

What if he meant the things he said?

What if he could love her?

With her eyes focused on the path in front of her, and her mind in a distant place, she failed to notice the swishing of orange skirts that approached her from behind.

"Miss Grace, is it?" A high-pitched voice said. "Grace Weston?"

Grace turned to her left, jerked from her musing by the round eyes of Miss Darby, holding a purring cat in her arms. Although similar in age and proportion to Grace, the two shared several differences. Miss Darby had blonde, tightly curled hair, with striking blue eyes. She dressed with the obvious intent to gather attention, manifested in her choice of an orange gown trimmed in yellow ribbon. Grace did not know her well, but in the few interactions they had shared, she knew that Miss Darby adored gossip.

"May I walk with you?" Miss Darby asked.

Grace nodded, confused at the woman's sudden interest in her. "How do you do, Miss Darby?"

"I am quite well." Miss Darby's voice betrayed her words as she followed Grace up the path. She clearly was not well. Her brow tightened in deep concern. "I could not help but observe that you just departed from the seaside where you shared a rather romantic moment with the future Earl of Coventry." She stroked her cat, one eyebrow cocked.

A romantic moment? Grace had stopped him from kissing her, which burned her insides with regret. Her self-discipline was running thin of late. "You are mistaken. We are merely… acquaintances. I was there on the beach to attend to his sister. Lord Ramsbury knows I will never enter a courtship with him."

Miss Darby brushed back the curls the wind had untethered from her hair. "I am glad to hear it. For I would hate for you to be hurt."

"Why should I be hurt?" Grace asked.

Miss Darby sighed. "I witnessed a very similar exchange just yesterday. My dear friend Miss Reed has been receiving extensive attention from his lordship. Lord Ramsbury stood with her on the sand, right where you so recently stood…" she lowered her voice to a whisper. "and he kissed her. I thought you might like to know. I hoped to one day marry him myself, but not if he is such a cad."

Grace's heart sunk, a heavy stone of ache crashing to her stomach. "Are you certain it was him?"

"Unfortunately, yes. I was as distraught as you are. I never thought Miss Reed to be so improper." Miss Darby buried her face in the fur of her cat, as if to hide her emotion. They continued to walk up the path, which had now blurred like a wet painting.

"He kissed her?" Grace's voice was numb.

"Thoroughly," she said, her voice muffled in her cat's fur.

Grace walked in silence, her face and heart on fire.

Miss Darby looked up from her cat. "I am sorry to have disturbed you so greatly. I thought it right to put an end to his deceit."

Grace looked up, blinking hard against the emotions that tore through her body, bringing tears to the back of her eyes. "Thank you," she said in a quick voice.

Miss Darby shook her head ruefully. "Men like Lord Ramsbury are not to be trusted."

Grace hardly heard her. Anger coiled and sprung inside her, flooding her face with heat. It was quickly replaced by pain—deep and searing—stinging in her heart and reaching out to every part of her.

How had she been such a fool?

She had let him make her feel special, if even for the briefest moment. Though she denied it, she had thought he might have been earnest. But Lord Ramsbury was as she had always suspected, a vile, shameless man who did not care for the emotions of others. He was treating Grace as a plaything while he pursued a marriage with another woman, one he knew would be foolish enough to accept him before his father's death.

Grace took a quaking breath, fighting tears once again. Dread pounded through her, sinking and sinking until she could hardly breathe.

"I will leave you. I am sorry to have upset you so." Miss Darby gave her an apologetic look.

Grace shook her head hard. "My heart is not broken. I never cared for that odious man. Just as he never cared for me."

"He is a collector of hearts. I suspect he finds pleasure in breaking them."

Grace didn't doubt those words.

When Miss Darby turned at the bend leading to her

own house, Grace finished her walk alone. She fought against her tears. Edward was not worth a single one.

He had not changed. She had so hoped he had. She steadied herself with deep breathing, moving with fast steps. The wind picked up speed, whipping against her skin and hair and dress.

When she reached her family's property line, she tossed the Shrewsbury cakes behind her, sickened at the thought of eating them. And she ran. She ran across the overgrown grass, through the back door, and up the stairs to her bedchamber. Once the door was firmly closed, her tears flowed freely down her cheeks. What had started as her own game had been won. Edward had fooled her into believing that he could love her. That he truly wished to marry her, and her alone. That he would flirt with her, and only her, for all of his life. What a lie that had been.

She stopped in front of her looking glass, wiping angrily at her wet cheeks. She would not be fooled a third time. Never.

And if she could help it, she would never see him again.

# Chapter 13

Edward arose early the next morning, breathing in the bright spring air as he walked to the gardens of Clemsworth. His mood had been elevated since the afternoon before, when he had had the privilege of seeing Grace—laughing with her and teasing her and earning a few rare smiles. Juliet had been unable to stop speaking of her for the entire evening, and at dinner, his mother had listened intently to the events of their day, eager to hear the outcome of Edward's next proposal.

The time had come. But the idea of asking her again sent his heart racing with fear. He had never been one to doubt himself, but with the possibility of losing Grace, he was struck with terror. How could he marry any other woman now? He couldn't. Grace Weston had irrevocably stolen his heart.

He could only guess—hope—that he had stolen hers

too. He took a deep breath, straightening his cravat. The white rose bush stood in front of him, nearly in full bloom. He touched the closest bud, lifting the shears he had stolen from the groundskeeper. He began clipping, gathering a handful of roses.

Something sharp punctured his thumb. He drew a quick breath, pulling his hand back. Blood seeped from the place where a thorn had cut him. He covered the abrasion with his other hand, cradling the roses in his arm. Thankfully his jacket was thick enough to withstand them.

He returned to the house to wrap the flowers. He could not have Grace being hurt by the thorns. On his way back outside, he picked up the book of Shakespeare's sonnets he had studied the night before. He had chosen the perfect one to share with Grace, and he was eager to see her reaction.

He had planned to make his proposal in the afternoon, but he could not wait. He would likely burst with anticipation, and fear would stop him if he waited much longer. He did not like the vulnerability Grace stirred up inside him. It terrified him.

Walking toward Weston Manor, he planned his words carefully. He could not ruin it this time. He feared it would be his last chance.

When he arrived on the part of the path that crossed behind the house, he considered turning back. He ran his hand over his hair in frustration, pacing over the cobblestones. He had never been so unsure of himself, so blasted cowardly.

*Walk.*

His feet obeyed, leading him around the border of the back property toward the front of the house. He froze when he saw something move beneath a tree near the stables.

Grace.

She held an embroidery hoop in one hand, scowling down at the needle as she meticulously stitched. She was wrapped up in a peach shawl to keep warm under the cloudy sky. She looked nothing short of adorable.

His heart crashed in his chest, harder than seawater against the shore. He willed himself to be confident as he walked toward her, reminding himself to smile. He was glad to see her outside. His first proposal had been in the drawing room, and had not brought about the results he had wanted. He considered her presence outside to be a stroke of luck.

A ray of morning light had recently broke through the clouds, bringing out golden tones in her brown hair. He watched as she took another stitch, still oblivious to his approach. As he came closer, she glanced up. Her eyes flew open wide and her shoulders tightened.

He offered his broadest smile. "Good morning, Grace. I am pleased and not at all surprised to find you here. But I would have predicted you to be holding a book."

She drew a deep breath, her expression guarded, bordering on angry. After the initial surprise faded, she glared at him. "Why are you here?" Her voice came out soft, broken, a contradiction to the anger in her features. She wrapped the shawl tighter around her, coming to her feet in one swift motion.

He didn't know how he had expected her to react, but this certainly wasn't it. He took a step closer. She had acted cold before. It was how she defended herself against his charm. Yes. That was all this was.

He laughed to dispel the unrest within him. "May I at

least give you these?" He extended the bouquet of white roses, raising one eyebrow. "I know they are your favorite."

She stared at the flowers, keeping her hands wrapped beneath her shawl, her breathing increasing in rate. She made no move to accept the flowers.

*Strange.*

He dropped to his knees, holding them out to her. "I know I am incorrigible and barely tolerable." He smiled, hoping to pull one from her. "But I have lost my heart to you, Miss Grace Weston. I have come to ask if you will please reconsider the request I once made." He breathed deeply. "I have come to ask, once again, if you will marry me."

She remained silent, her eyes distant and guarded, her lips pressed together.

His stomach twisted. What had he done wrong this time? He felt his hope dissipating inside him. When her silence persisted, he stood, letting the flowers drop to his side.

A tear escaped from her carefully stoic expression. She wiped her cheek angrily, turning her back to him.

"Grace." He walked around her, his heart stalling. He stared at her face, trying to puzzle out her aloofness. Her brown eyes looked anywhere but at him. What had he done to make her cry? Dread poured through him. These were not tears of joyful acceptance.

She sniffed, shaking her head. "No. I will not marry you."

He cupped the side of her face, pulling her eyes to his. "You do not mean that."

Her eyes flashed with hesitation before hardening. "I do."

"Grace," he wiped away another tear that fell on her soft cheek, wetting her lashes.

She pushed him away, taking several steps back. "Do not try to convince me otherwise. I know you do not care for me as you pretend to. You have lied to me enough."

He filled the space she had created, frustration rising within him. "I do not understand."

"I am finished being fooled by you. My mind cannot be changed."

"Nor can mine." He tipped his head down. "I chose you. I chose you the moment I saw you in the woods. At that time, I confess I chose you because I was desperate to find a wife, and I was short on time. After you refused me, I continued to pursue you because of my pride. I could not bear being rejected again. But," he touched her arms gently, turning her toward him. "as I came to know you… I came to realize that if I lost you it would be more than my pride that would be bruised. You are bold, spirited, determined, and you are unafraid of your own voice—you speak what you wish." He brushed back a strand of hair that stuck to her wet cheek. "You are beautiful in every way."

She stared at the ground, wrapping her shawl tighter. "You are right. I do speak what I wish, and I will do so now," she said in a quiet voice. "I wish to never see you again. I wish that you had never passed me in the woods, and that you had never asked me to marry you." She looked up, the fierceness in her eyes forcing Edward back a step. Her voice hardened. "I would lose a thousand wagers before I would be foolish enough to believe you, and foolish enough to marry you." She turned around again.

He felt as if he had been struck squarely in the chest. Her words hung between them, taut with misunderstanding. Why had he allowed himself to care for her? Had he not learned his lesson the last time he risked his heart for a woman? Pain spread through his limbs like fire, coursing through his veins. He meant to offer an angry rebuke, but all he felt was emptiness.

Cold emptiness.

He swallowed hard, forcing his emotions to a safer place. Without speaking another word, he retreated from her, his throat burning. The first time she had rejected him his pride had stung for days. His pride was unaffected this time, relaying the burden of her rejection to every other part of him instead.

He tossed the book of sonnets beside the roses on the grass, turning his back to her. What had happened to make her so upset? He could think of nothing. Just the day before they had parted ways in good standing.

He passed the Weston's gardens, coming upon a large, overgrown bush.

A distant gasp hit his ears from behind, and he turned. Where he stood hidden from view by the large bushes, Mrs. Weston did not see him as she approached her daughter with hurried steps. Her voice, loud and shrill, sounded very similar to Grace's voice when she had first been vying for his proposal. "Grace! How dare you reject him again?"

Edward stepped farther behind the bush, keeping himself hidden as he listened.

"Mama—you do not understand."

"No, it is *you* who does not understand. Lord Ramsbury is soon to inherit Clemsworth and a series of smaller estates in Yorkshire. Do you realize how much property will be in his possession? And his wealth is beyond any man in Brighton. I thought I explained our situation to you in terms that you could understand. You must marry as soon as you are able, and to a man that will provide you with an adequate living. Lord Ramsbury's holdings are more than adequate. We simply cannot sustain you and Harriett for much longer."

"I know, Mama."

"Then why, pray tell, did you refuse him?"

"I will not marry a man that does not truly love me."

Edward grumbled, stopping himself from marching out from the bush to deny her statement.

"If he doesn't love you then what reason could he possibly have for proposing?"

"He is being forced to marry by his father in order to keep his inheritance."

Her mother scoffed. "But the laws of primogeniture cannot be so easily surpassed. I have scarcely heard of such a thing."

"It is true."

"Then you must catch him while he is so desperate! The opportunity will pass you by. He has still chosen you."

"He is amusing himself with me until another woman accepts his hand. He does not love me."

A long sigh. "It is the books again, isn't it?"

"What?"

"You have been reading again. My dear, those are fictional stories. Love is a novelty in marriage, a rare treasure, but few ever find it. There are more important matters to consider. Here you have a man of considerable wealth that has asked you a *second* time to marry him. You are to find Lord Ramsbury at once and revoke your rejection."

"I cannot." Her voice came out weaker, as if she were considering it.

"Please, Grace. It is your father's dearest wish to have to provided for. Think of the wealth and prestige of a countess. And think of how envious cousin Prudence will be."

An extended moment of hesitation followed, and the dread in Edward's stomach grew. All his life he had been desired for his possessions. He thought Grace would be different. If she accepted him now, it would only be for his holdings, not his heart. He pushed back the sorrow that threatened to envelop him. Why had he expected anything more?

"I will—I will consider it."

"Very well. Good heavens, child. I thought Harriett to be the most difficult to manage, but you have surpassed her."

Silence followed, telling Edward that Mrs. Weston had traveled back to the house.

He steadied his breathing and tightened his jaw. There had been a time that Edward thought of marriage as nothing more than a business settlement. But the idea of that now filled him with unending trepidation. Business was meant to deal with money, marriage was not. Marriage was meant to deal with love. But such were the ways of society, that the latter was a rarity.

However, since meeting Grace, he had begun to share her sentiments on the idea of marriage. He would not marry someone that did not love him. He couldn't bear the thought of marrying her, of loving her, only to know that she loved his wealth more.

But soon his father would be dead, and he would be without wealth, and without Grace. He choked on a surge of grief, curling his fists as he walked back to Clemsworth. She had already told him she never wished to see him again. And he would certainly not make an effort to see her only to offer his possessions. But which fate was worse? A life with his inheritance and a fortune-hunter wife, or a life with nothing?

He would not give her the opportunity to find him today, to revoke her rejection. She had already made her decision.

# Chapter 14

Watching her mother's retreating form, Grace wrapped her arms around herself, raw emotion clutching at her throat. How could she do as her mother said? How could she agree to marry Edward after knowing what Miss Darby had revealed to her? Grace could not forget the look of seriousness in her mother's eyes when she had discussed her need to marry well. Was her mother right? Was Grace a fool not to take such an offer? If she could remove her heart from the situation it would be much easier. But it was too late for that.

She picked up the book Edward had cast onto the ground, brushing away bits of grass from the cover. A deep burgundy ribbon hung out from a marked page. She opened to it, her eyes sweeping over the words she had not given Edward a chance to read.

*Let me not to the marriage of true minds*
*Admit impediments. Love is not love*
*Which alters when it alteration finds,*
*Or bends with the remover to remove:*
*O no! it is an ever-fixed mark*
*That looks on tempests and is never shaken;*
*It is the star to every wandering bark,*
*Whose worth's unknown, although his height be taken*
*Love's not Time's fool, though rosy lips and cheeks*
*Within his bending sickle's compass come:*
*Love alters not with his brief hours and weeks,*
*But bears it out even to the edge of doom.*
*If this be error and upon me proved,*
*I never writ, nor no man ever loved.*

She blinked her tears away, snapping the book closed and holding it to her chest. The beauty of Shakespeare's words rang through her heart, filling it with melancholy and reflection. How could Edward have dared read those words to her? He didn't love her. He was as she had always suspected—pretending.

Her heart stung with betrayal and regret as she walked inside on shaking legs. She had not spoken to Harriett the day before after speaking with Miss Darby. In fact, Grace had closed herself in her room for the entire evening, speaking to no one but their maid, who had sensed something was amiss as she removed the pins from Grace's hair. She had not even gone to dinner, feigning a cold.

When Harriett had retired for the evening in the room they shared, Grace had pretended to be asleep. She didn't trust herself to relay her exchange with Miss Darby without a show of tears. She couldn't let Harriett see how foolish she had been to care so deeply.

Steeling herself, Grace pushed through the back door of the house, still clutching the book of sonnets. She closeted her emotions, willing her heart to slow and her legs to quit their shaking. She wanted to feel angry that Edward had deceived her, but instead she only felt increasing sorrow.

On her way up the stairs, she was stopped by her sister's voice, echoing in the entry hall.

"Grace! Are you feeling well again?"

Grace paused her ascent, drawing a deep breath before turning around. Harriett stood with one hand on the banister, staring up at her. She wore a puce chiffon gown, a selection more suited to a ball than to a morning at home. When she saw Grace's expression, hers immediately shifted to one of deep concern. "What has happened?"

Grace felt her chin contract, a sign of coming tears. She slumped against the banister as Harriett hurried up the stairs. Grace swallowed, forcing herself to remain composed. "Much has happened."

Harriett placed on hand on her shoulder. "Do tell me."

Releasing a sigh, Grace stared down at the marble floor beneath the staircase, the sun glaring upon it through the windows. "Lord Ramsbury just proposed again."

Harriett gasped. "Did you accept?"

Grace shook her head, turning away from Harriett's disapproving gaze.

"Why ever not?" her sister asked, her voice heavy with dismay.

"Lord Ramsbury has not changed as I hoped. He is not genuine in his affection, or at least I am not the sole receiver of it. He is simply eager to marry to keep his fortune, and that is all. I have been a fool, Harriett."

Her sister frowned. "What has led you to this conclusion?"

"I suspected it from the beginning, but Miss Darby found me on my walk home yesterday afternoon. My suspicions were confirmed by our conversation." Grace made her voice hard in an attempt to hide the tremor within it.

"Miss Darby? The eldest, Lydia?"

Grace nodded. Harriett was further acquainted with the Darbys than Grace, as Miss Lydia Darby was closer to her in age, and the two had spent much time together in their youth.

Harriett clutched Grace's shoulder more tightly, an urgency in her grasp. "What did she say to you?"

Grace did not want to dwell on the words again. They had left a deep hole inside her. "She witnessed Lord Ramsbury and me on the beach with Juliet," Grace said, her voice strained. "She saw our… overly familiar interactions. Then she told me that she had seen Lord Ramsbury just the day before, sharing a kiss with Miss Reed."

Grace waited for a gasp to come from Harriett, some indication that she was appalled by the news, but she simply stared, eyes wide. "I would not have suspected Miss Darby to be that despicable."

"Miss Darby?" Grace shook her head. "It was not a despicable act at all. I am glad she told me what she witnessed."

"How could you have possibly believed her?" Harriett could not conceal her shock.

"Should I not?"

"You most certainly should not." Harriett lowered her voice. "Miss Darby will do anything to keep Lord Ramsbury from marrying any other woman besides herself. She fancies herself madly in love with him. She is an untruthful woman, Grace. Her word is not to be trusted."

A wave of confusion struck her. "Why would she invent such a dreadful story?"

"Because in her spying on you and Lord Ramsbury, she realized his intentions toward you and hoped to stop them." Harriett's cheeks fumed with anger. "How despicable."

Grace considered her sister's explanation, desperately wanting it to be true. "How can I be certain? In my acquaintance with her, she has not given me a reason to distrust her. Lord Ramsbury has. I am better off believing her than him, am I not?"

"Trust my judgement," Harriett said. "I am certain Miss Darby's words to you were a direct lie."

Grace's heart thudded, hope rising within her. No. She could not allow it. She had just rejected Edward a second time. Whether Miss Darby's words were true or not, Edward would never propose again. He would likely never wish to see her again, just as she had told him. Her opportunity was passed.

"But I do not know for certain," Grace whispered, her voice too weak for anything more. "I cannot rely on a guess or suspicion."

Harriett chewed one nail, deep thought in her eyes. "We will discover the truth. But you must know, from what I have witnessed, I suspect Lord Ramsbury is quite in love with you."

Grace fiddled with a loose thread on her gown. "How do you know?"

Harriett was silent for a long moment before she shrugged. "Truth is shown in the actions of people, not in their words. Miss Darby has shown herself to be dishonest and spiteful in all the time I have known her. Her words to you should therefore mean nothing. Lord Ramsbury professes to wish to marry you because he cares for you. Has he shown you that he cares for you, or has he only spoken it?"

Grace searched her mind for the answer. One question had haunted her since the moment Edward arrived on the property this morning: if Edward didn't care for her at all, then why did he continue to propose? Could he not give up and choose a new lady—even Miss Reed?

Her thoughts spun too rapidly to formulate a response. Harriett smiled. "Do not lose hope. The ball at Pengrave is in one week. We have received our invitation and I am certain many Brighton families will be in attendance as well. You will see Lord Ramsbury there. The two of you may then sort out your feelings."

Grace shook her head hard, panic rising within her. "No. I cannot face him again. Not after I so harshly rejected him." She still did not know if he could be trusted or not. She couldn't risk seeing his blue eyes, hearing his voice, allowing herself to be deceived again.

"Please, Grace. You must go!"

Grace sighed. "I will consider it."

"I suppose this week will be a test of his devotion. If he is not engaged to another woman by the ball, and is still set on you, then we will know for certain."

"How can anything be certain?" Grace let out a long sigh, dragging her fingers over her cheeks.

"If he asked you again to marry him, what would be your response?"

"I do not know. But I doubt he will ask again. If he does, I will have little choice in the matter. Mama was very disappointed that I refused him."

Harriett's eyebrows rose. "Is that why she came marching inside as if she had just seen the devil himself?"

"I'm afraid so."

"I do see her wisdom," Harriett said. "He is wealthy and handsome."

"But he does not love me."

"Stop saying that, Grace! Perhaps you have not seen it, but I have. He looks at you as if you are… an angel descended from the heavens. Or as I would look at a new bonnet made of the finest fabrics and lace of the continent."

A smile slipped past Grace's fear. But only for a moment. Did she dare attend the ball? Her stomach turned at the thought. But she had a week to prepare, to determine if she had the courage.

Harriett giggled. "And you look at him as if he is a Shrewsbury cake."

"Harriett!" Grace covered her face, a cursed blush burning her cheeks. "I do not."

"You do indeed."

Grace peeked through her fingers, her sister's smile infectious.

Harriett's laughter subsided. "I will speak to Miss Darby if you wish. Or as an even more reliable source, I will speak with Miss Reed."

Grace gave a slow nod. If Harriett spoke to Miss Reed casually about the matter, she could decipher the truth.

"They will both be in attendance at the ball, to be sure. I will make certain to speak with Miss Reed directly."

"Thank you, Harriett," Grace said. A small part of her now burned with hope, something she had been lacking before meeting her sister here and learning of Miss Darby's potential deception. Doubt still thrived in great quantity, but even the smallest bit of hope had a way of dispelling it.

"At any rate, I have little choice but to help you," Harriett said. "I am responsible for suggesting our wager, which has placed you in this plight. My conscience would not allow me to stand by and watch you suffer."

"Then I suppose it is your conscience that deserves my gratitude."

Harriett laughed. "My conscience thanks you."

Grace started up the stairs again, her steps feeling much lighter than when she had entered the house. Would Edward attempt to see her before the ball? No. She had asked him not to see her. Had her words actually struck him? Her mind flashed with the memory of his face, the defeat she had seen in his features. It was true what Harriett said—Grace would need to watch his actions. As she considered his recent actions toward her, she found that they contradicted Miss Darby's claim.

But pretending was one of Edward's strengths.

Her head ached as she closed the door of her bedchamber behind her. It would be a long week, to be sure.

# Chapter 15

A familiar feeling settled in Edward's chest each morning when he awoke. He thought he had abandoned it, but it had returned, destructive and painful. Ever since Grace had rejected him five days before, he had wrestled with the returning feelings of loss, regret, and an utter absence of hope.

He groaned as he sat up in bed, pushing his hair from his forehead. How could he carry on like this? It had been several days, and he felt himself slipping back to the habits that had brought his father to the decision to disinherit him. He had spent the night before in the library with a bottle of brandy, and had only found his way to his bedchamber with the help of Henry.

Edward rubbed his head. This was wrong. He would not allow it to happen again. He would be the man his mother and sister expected him to be. He would fulfill his role.

But his father was dying rapidly, and the thought of finding a different woman to marry filled him with aching dread. But Grace had made herself clear. She hated him, just as she had always said.

He came to his feet, cringing at the pounding in his head. He had allowed Miss Buxton's rejection to bring him to a pitiful state such as this. He couldn't let Grace do it too. His heart stung at the thought of her.

The loss of Miss Buxton now felt like a distant memory, a faint and shallow wound. Even as he considered the feelings he endured at her rejection when it was fresh, they did not compare at all to the depth of hurt Grace had inflicted on him.

What had he done wrong? He still had no explanation for her sudden coldness toward him. The contrast from the day before his proposal was stark, and he could not decipher why. Twice he had almost ventured to her house again to beg for an explanation.

Readying himself quickly, he called upon his valet to quicken the process. He had been spending his days with Juliet, who needed him now more than ever. Juliet had surely been confused at Edward's distant behavior over the last several days.

He refused to become to Juliet how their father had been all their lives.

Edward made his way down the stairs, finding his sister in the drawing room with a thick book. She wore her father's spectacles as she read, though she didn't need them. The image reminded him of Grace, and his heart stung all over again. He smiled at her from the doorway, surprised to see Henry and their mother beside her.

Henry's eyes lifted, settling on Edward with a look of disapproval. "I hope you have a cutting headache."

"Thank you for your concern," Edward said with a soft smile. "Not to worry. I have abandoned the drink. I will not become once again the dreadful creature I was."

His mother glanced up with a weary smile before returning her focus to Juliet's book, from which she read aloud in a quiet voice.

"I am glad to hear it." Henry patted the brocade sofa. "Sit."

Edward obeyed, eyebrows raised.

"Have you found a new woman to pursue?"

The dread in Edward's stomach surged. "No. I do not plan to."

His mother stopped reading, leaning around her daughter to touch Edward's knee. "Your father insists upon it. There is little time. I do not wish to see you endure the scrutiny that a disinheritance would bring upon you." She gave him a gentle glance. "I am very sorry that Miss Grace will not marry you. I know how difficult it has been for you. But there is still time for you to find a new woman, one that will be willing and enthusiastic at the thought of being your wife."

He recalled Grace's conversation with her own mother outside the stables. Grace had seemed to consider changing her mind, but only for his wealth. If he asked her again, would her answer be different? He felt as though he at least needed an explanation. He drew a heavy breath. "Perhaps you are right. I ought to give up."

Henry's eyes rounded. "I have never known you to surrender."

"That is because my pride would not allow it. Miss Grace Weston trampled my pride and tore it into thousands of pieces." He smiled, but it never reached his eyes.

"Oh, my dear." His mother touched his cheek affectionately. "Grieving a loss is never easy. I will grieve your father, but eventually I must carry on with the life I have been given. You may grieve Miss Grace, but you too must carry on."

Edward nodded slowly, swallowing the lump in his throat. "Who might I pursue instead?"

His mother sat back, rubbing her chin. "Miss Rose Daventry is a pretty young lady with a respectable family."

He groaned. "No. That is who Grace suggested."

"Very well." She glanced heavenward, her forehead tightening in thought. "You might consider Miss Elizabeth Reed? I know she is the eldest and her family is quite eager to have her married. She is a quiet sort of girl, fairly pretty, with many accomplishments to note. Her mother is a dear friend of mine."

A quiet sort of girl was precisely what Edward needed. Anything else would remind him too much of Grace. He sighed. "When might I see this Miss Reed?"

"I am certain she will be in attendance at the ball at Pengrave in two days. I will ensure you are introduced."

He pushed back his reluctance, reminding himself that this was necessary. "Very well." His voice was curt, hiding the emotions within him. He stood from the sofa, the room suddenly too stuffy to breathe. With a quick farewell, he departed, stopping in the hallway. He tightened his jaw and fisted his hands. He had once been looking forward to the ball at Pengrave, the residence of his friend, Philip.

But now he couldn't wait until it was over.

The ride to Pengrave was longer than Edward had expected, giving him far too much time to worry. He stared out the window, his usual smile long absent. The carriage moved over the uneven path, causing his knees to bounce against Henry's, who sat across from him. Their mother had stayed with their father and Juliet, leaving her sons to represent their family at the ball.

Nothing sounded quite as terrible as dancing at the moment, and Edward's heart pounded with the possibility of seeing Grace. He was supposed to be pursuing Miss Reed, for his mother had appointed a mutual acquaintance to introduce them, and he was to claim her first dance.

His skull throbbed with a renewed headache as the interior lighting of Pengrave came into view, candles flickering brightly through the windows. Since the marriage of Lord and Lady Seaford, they had yet to host such a grand ball, and all of Brighton had been looking forward to it. The grounds were full of people who stared up in awe at the tall, haunting estate as they crossed the grass to the entrance.

Edward lacked the energy to portray his usual public appearance, keeping a serious expression instead. Society would surely understand, as it was common knowledge that his father's death was near. They did not need to know that the most prominent reason for his stoic expression was a broken heart.

When he and Henry reached the interior of the home, they were ushered toward the ballroom. He stopped with his brother in the crowded entry hall. The ballroom was already filled to near capacity with guests, many faces familiar among them. Edward found himself searching for Grace before stopping himself.

As they made their way through the ballroom doors, a tall head of dark curls came into view above the crowd. Philip Honeyfield, the recent marquess, gave a wide smile as he stepped through the crowd to meet Edward. His wife, Lady Seaford, clung to his arm, her petite frame easily swallowed up in the crowd.

"Lord Ramsbury, welcome to Pengrave! And welcome, Mr. Beaumont." He turned to Edward. "I must confess I did not think you would come."

Edward laughed, a sound he hadn't heard himself make in days. Philip had not seen him for over a month, a time when he had been in his most pitiful state. Edward greeted Lady Seaford with a nod before turning his attention back to Philip. "I couldn't miss witnessing your humiliation," he said. "How could a man as ungainly as yourself host a successful ball?"

Philip chuckled, pulling his wife closer. "I could not. You have your hostess to thank for the preparations."

She colored slightly, the red of her cheeks a softer shade than her red hair. "I thought it right to host a ball to introduce us to society. A spring ball was the perfect opportunity, for Philip loves spring."

A new voice came from behind Edward, one he recognized. Adam Claridge stepped around him, moving to greet Philip. Edward turned, his eyes falling on Amelia, the former Miss Buxton. She looked up at him, her brown eyes darting away almost instantly. Adam stopped when he saw Edward, a hardness forming in his gaze.

Henry exchanged a look of concern with Edward, knowing full well that this was the woman who had broken Edward's heart the previous year.

Edward knew why Adam Claridge was not fond of him. The year before, Adam's sister Eleanor had entered a secret marriage with a man of the regiment, leaving her family to wonder where she had gone. As a friend of the officer, Edward had been sworn to secrecy on their whereabouts. In Adam's search, he had enlisted Amelia to help glean information from Edward, which had been the only reason she had pretended to have an interest in him.

Adam still seemed to blame Edward for his sister's disappearance, but much of his dislike also came from Edward's former adoration of his wife.

Edward glanced at Amelia again, his gaze flickering to her hand, resting on her growing belly. She avoided his gaze, guilt over her deceit still hovering in her features. He examined his heart for any attachment to her, any sorrow over seeing her with Mr. Claridge, but felt nothing. All he felt within his heart was a longing for Grace—the pain of losing her.

"Good evening, Mr. Claridge. Mrs. Claridge." Edward kept his voice polite, no bitterness within him. He turned to Adam, who regarded him coldly. "I hope my information leading to your sister found you well. I apologize sincerely for withholding it. I could not betray my friend."

Adam cleared his throat. "I have not received word from Eleanor since last summer."

Edward frowned. "She has not written at all? Have you met her husband?"

"No."

Amelia touched Adam's arm, whispering something to him. His expression softened, and he gave Edward a curt nod before turning away, engaging Lord and Lady Seaford in conversation once again.

Amelia stepped forward, hesitant and slow. "I hope

you understand, my lord, that I am very sorry for my deceit. I should not have led you to believe…" her voice trailed off and she looked down at the floor.

He gave her a soft smile. "I forgive you. You acted in behalf of the man you loved," he nodded toward Adam. "I too have done foolish things for love." His eyes lifted, settling across the room, where Grace stood with her sister, her gaze surveying the crowd. His stomach turned over.

Until Amelia spoke again, he had nearly forgotten she stood before him. She smiled, a weight lifting from her eyes. "Thank you. I wish you every happiness, my lord."

"You as well." He dropped his head in a nod, bidding her farewell. She returned to her husband's side. The two spoke with Philip for a moment before disappearing into the crowd. Henry became engaged in conversation with a gentleman of his acquaintance, leaving Edward alone with Lord and Lady Seaford.

Philip raised his eyebrows, stepping toward Edward once more. "You endured that encounter quite well. I am impressed."

Edward shook his head. "I no longer feel any affection for Amelia."

Philip's eyes widened. "And what has brought about this change?"

He looked down, suddenly embarrassed to be speaking with *Philip Honeyfield* on such matters. "I have been foolish enough to fall in love."

"Ah… a foolish endeavor indeed."

Lady Seaford pinched his arm, a playful scowl on her brow.

He laughed, staring down at her. "But a worthy one." Philip's eyes raised to Edward. "Who is this lady? Is an engagement on the rise?"

"No."

"And why not?"

Edward sighed. He didn't know why he felt the need to explain the situation to Philip. "It is a lengthy tale, my friend. You must save time to converse with your other guests."

"Now I am very curious."

"As am I," Lady Seaford agreed.

Edward rubbed one side of his face. The eager eyes of both Philip and his wife stared at him. They would not be satisfied with anything but the truth. So he relayed it all, from the day he first found Grace in the woods to the day he proposed a second time.

Philip did not hide his dismay throughout much of the story, shaking his head in wonder as Edward finished.

"I—er—" Philip laughed. "That is quite the quandary."

"What shall I do?" Edward said, not appreciating the humor Philip found in the situation.

Philip cocked his head back. "Are *you* asking *me* for advice?"

"Yes," Edward grumbled.

Philip chuckled, thoroughly amused by the notion. When he had first received word that he was to become a marquess, he had come to Edward for advice on how to behave in society as a titled gentleman, and how to woo the woman on his arm. Edward's advice had obviously worked in Philip's favor, as the public seemed to adore him, just as his wife did.

"Very well." Philip squared his shoulders, far too pleased with Edward's request. "She obviously doubts your devotion."

"Yes. But I cannot imagine why. I have been quite

clear." He sighed in frustration. "But it does not matter. I plan to find a different woman to marry before my father's death." He kept his voice low to ensure he would not be overheard.

"You cannot do that!" Philip said. "Do not give up! You must keep your inheritance *and* the woman you love. There will be no compromise."

Edward stared ahead, his gaze finding Grace once again. Her eyes met his across the room, a blush racing across her cheeks before she looked away. She couldn't be indifferent, he knew it. Then why did she refuse him? The question baffled him.

Philip leaned forward. "Have you kissed her?" he asked in a low voice.

"Philip!" his wife said. "You mustn't encourage such a thing. And certainly not with so many guests that may hear you."

He grinned.

Edward narrowed his eyes, refusing to admit that no, he had not. But he did not need *Philip Honeyfield* encouraging him to kiss Grace. He did not need any encouragement. If a kiss is what could change her mind, then devil take it, he would kiss her, no matter the consequence.

A woman with a bronze turban and tightly curled hair stepped up beside Edward, offering a bow. He recognized her immediately from the hours she had spent at Clemsworth for tea with his mother.

"Good evening, Mrs. Reed," he said. "Allow me to introduce you to Lord and Lady Seaford."

She gave a deep nod, her smile wide with excitement as she regarded them. "I thank you for your kindness in extending your invitation to my family."

Lady Seaford returned her smile.

Mrs. Reed returned her attention to Edward. Only then did he notice the young lady hovering behind her, auburn curls twisted in a knot atop her head, little pearls mixed among them. The young lady looked down at the ground as she stepped forward, her eyes darting around as if she were terrified to be seen near him. Only then did Edward notice Miss Darby, standing several feet behind, shooting daggers at Miss Reed's back with her gaze, her hand wrapped dangerously tight around a champagne flute.

"Come now, my dear," Mrs. Reed scowled, tugging her daughter forward by the elbow. "Might I make known to you, my lord, my eldest daughter, Miss Elizabeth Reed."

Edward smiled to be polite, but the idea of pursuing Miss Reed now felt completely implausible. When he had met Grace's eyes across the room, he had seen that she was not indifferent. She was afraid, she was doubtful, but not indifferent. Mingled with Philip's words of encouragement, Edward felt his hope lifting again, despite all odds.

He had promised Miss Reed a dance, so a dance he would give. But the moment it was over he would find Grace.

He would discover the truth of her aloofness toward him.

And he would make certain she knew, without a doubt, the truth of his feelings toward her.

## Chapter 16

"Perhaps it is not as it seems," Harriett said in an attempt to console her sister.

Grace watched as Lord Ramsbury led Miss Reed to the center of the ballroom at the start of the quadrille, a tight ball of dread forming in her stomach.

"Perhaps he is simply being kind. She *was* in need of a partner." Harriett chewed her lip as she followed Grace's gaze. It seemed even Harriett knew her explanations were in vain.

Grace swallowed back the emotion that rose in her throat. "It is not so. Miss Darby's words have practically been proven." Her voice sounded unfamiliar to her own ears, broken and defeated. "I should not have come."

"Do not say that, Grace. We might still make the evening enjoyable. You must find another gentleman of your acquaintance to dance with. Henry Beaumont, perhaps? Then we might see if it stirs up envy in Lord Ramsbury."

Grace shook her head. "I am finished with this game. I will not be a player in it any longer."

Harriett sighed. "I shall speak to Miss Darby directly. I will coerce the truth out of her, even if I must threaten one of her precious cats to do it."

"Do not. It is no longer necessary." Grace felt the rush of heartbreak, stinging in her chest and moving through her limbs, out to the tips of her fingers. She had never been special, and she had never been wanted. She was merely one of many, a single flower among a garden. Her eyes stung with tears as she watched Edward smile down at Miss Reed, turning and spinning to the lively music.

The song was drawing to a close. As much as she wanted to, she could not tear her gaze away from him. She had missed his teasing smiles and infectious laughter this week. She had spent the week before the ball keeping as busy as she could, trying to forget him. But all she had achieved was a greater longing for him. She had missed him terribly, and she hated herself for it.

His eyes, clear blue in the candlelight, met hers above the head of his partner. The last notes of the dance hung in the air, and he bowed to Miss Reed. When his head raised, his eyes found her again.

Unable to stay in the room for another moment, Grace muttered an unintelligible excuse to her sister before threading through the crowd and out the ballroom door. She did not care how improper it was to be wandering the halls alone. She could not bear to see Edward share another dance, and another, with the other woman he had managed to trick.

She passed several paintings in the deserted halls as she rushed as far from the ballroom as possible. Distant footsteps grew faster behind her, becoming louder.

"Grace," a voice called.

Edward's voice.

She stiffened, catching her breath at a nearby doorway. Her throat constricted and her heart built a new barrier. She turned to face him, her pulse pounding in her ears.

Edward stopped several feet away, his eyes soft and careful. "Grace… where are you going?"

"Please keep your distance, my lord. We must not be seen together alone." She turned around, continuing her aimless walk down the vast hallway. His footsteps followed her, even faster this time. They rounded a corner near the lineage portraits, and Grace stopped. The short hall ended abruptly at a closed door, with no other place for her to turn.

"Look at me," he said, touching her shoulder. "Please."

She drew a heavy breath. To look at him now would be dangerous—detrimental to her plan to stay away from him, to not allow him to charm her into foolishness again. She remained firm in her conviction, facing the door.

His voice came again, soft, pleading. "I have been tormented this week by our last meeting. I must know why you refused me so plainly. What have I done to earn such a rejection?"

Crossing her arms, she retained as much fortitude as she was able before turning around. He tipped his head down to look at her, searching her eyes. The windows from the adjacent hall provided just enough moonlight to decipher his features, painted gray in the darkness, the glint of his eyes reflecting regret.

"You lied to me," she said, her voice cracking as tears escaped her. "I am not the only woman you flirt with. I am not the only one you wish to marry. Your game has not ended, and I believe it never shall. You are just as I suspected you to be—just as you were those years ago. You have no regard for my feelings, nor any qualms in toying with my heart. I will not be treated in such a way."

His brow contracted. He stepped forward, raising his hand to Grace's cheek, swiping away her tears. The action only brought more, choking her with quiet sobs.

"How can you not see that I am in love with you?"

Her eyes shot up to his. She wanted to believe it, desperately, but she didn't know how.

"You said you would lose a thousand wagers before you would marry me." He held her face between both his hands now. "I would lose my inheritance a thousand times before I would marry another. I will wait for you, Grace, as long as you require. I will spend my life trying to convince you if that is what I must do."

She shook her head, unable to speak past the tears that shook her.

His expression tightened. "There is something you are not telling me. Please." He smoothed back the hair that stuck to her cheeks.

What would he do if he discovered she knew of his scheme? Would he abandon her there in the hall and rush back to the arms of Miss Reed?

"I s-spoke to Miss Darby. She saw us by the w-water." Grace composed herself, her crossed arms pulling tighter. "She told me she saw you with Miss Reed the day before, and that you kissed her. And then I saw you at the ball, dancing with her, and I was certain that—"

He shook his head, his eyes wide. "That is not true. I did dance with Miss Reed, but that was the first time I had ever made her acquaintance."

"What?" Grace's voice was hushed.

Edward took her hands firmly in his. "I do not know

why Miss Darby would concoct such a story, but I assure you, it is not true. You have my word, Grace."

She studied his expression, her heart pounding. "How can I be certain of anything?" she asked, her voice hoarse.

"I am certain of many things," he said. "I am certain that I have no attachment to Miss Reed, nor any other lady, with the exception of you. I am certain that I love you, and that I wish to marry you." His eyebrows turned down, his mouth clenching as he clung to her hands. "I will only ask you one last time. If you still wish to be left alone, I will obey. I have much to offer you that will benefit your family and your own living. Even if that is all you desire, I still extend it to you. I only hope it will bring you the happiness you deserve, even if I cannot." He drew a breath, bringing her fingers to his lips. "But my sincerest hope is that you will have me, and all my faults, as your own. That you will come to love me."

Grace could scarcely breathe as she considered his words. As tempting as they were, her mind still burned with uncertainty. "How is your father's health?" she asked, her voice careful.

He appeared surprised by her change of subject. "He is predicted to live only a week longer, perhaps less."

"And so you have become desperate."

He dropped her hands, exhaling in exasperation. "I have never met a more stubborn—" He took a pace away from her, breathing deeply. "I do not know what else to say. I have poured my heart out to you, Grace. I have declared my love for you, yet it is not enough. Yes, my father is soon to die, but I will always want you. I would want you even if my father had placed no stipulation upon me."

Grace set her jaw. "You cannot know that for certain."

He raked his hand over his hair, half his mouth lifting in a smile of disbelief. "Are you refusing my proposal *again*?"

The air grew taut between them, and Grace shivered, craving the warmth of him, the comfort of his closeness. How could she refuse the option to have him near for her entire life? Even with unanswered questions, she could not refuse him. Not directly. But she could not trust her emotions at present. She needed time to realign them—apart from Edward and his piercing blue eyes. She released a quaking breath. "I will—I will consider it."

He stared at her, unblinking. "You will *consider* it? Have I not given you long enough to consider it?"

Defense rose within her, snapping like a whip. "At least I am not refusing."

"You are only considering it because you need my fortune, and your mother desires for you to be a countess." His voice was quiet, filled with hurt.

"No—"

"Do not deny it. I heard your conversation with your mother after my last proposal." His voice had hardened. "You see me as a relentless stealer of hearts, eager to break yours. You are afraid of that. And *my* greatest fear has always been to be loved only for my title and fortune."

Grace scowled. "A lady must consider such things when choosing a husband."

"Then your decision should be swift. If that is all you desire, then you ought to answer me now, before my father dies and I lose that which you desire."

Grace's breath shook on the way out, and she stopped the words she meant to say. Edward could be a fisherman and she would still love him.

Anger rose inside her at his assumptions of her character. She was not a fortune hunter; she was an advocate of love in a marriage, and that was why she feared marrying him. She could not decipher what was truth and what were lies. She was surrounded by an abundance of both.

"When may I expect your decision?" he grumbled.

Grace's mind raced with fear and hesitation. "In three days," she blurted.

"Three days?"

"Yes."

He bit the inside of his cheek, shaking his head. "You do enjoy torturing me."

She scowled. "No."

"Do not deny it." His words were slower and he walked toward her, filling the space between them.

Grace stepped back fast, clattering directly against the wooden door. She had forgotten how trapped she was. Her heart pounded as Edward stepped closer, tipping his head down.

She searched for her strength, but it was gone, stolen by the look in his eyes as he stared down at her, by the touch of his hands as they wrapped around her upper arms. "I would like to offer you one more thing to consider," he said.

She swallowed, looking away from his eyes. Her voice came more quickly than she intended. "I do not think that is necessary, actually, because I have all the information I require, and—"

Her words were stopped by Edward's lips as they captured hers, his kiss deliberate and slow as he took her face between his hands. She had scarcely recovered from the shock before Edward pulled back for air, his nose pressed against her cheek.

Before she could stop them, her hands clutched the

collar of his shirt, pulling his lips back to hers, first reluctant, then eager, kissing him until she couldn't breathe. He pressed her back against the door, his kiss growing deeper, firmer, more determined. He kissed her as if he would never kiss her again, a notion which Grace was now strongly opposed to.

Edward pulled away, as if by great effort, tracing his thumb over her cheek. She stared up at him in shock.

His eyes grew heavy as they roamed her face. "I hope you will consider that when making your decision."

He took her hand in his, bringing her fingertips to his lips one last time before stepping away.

Her heart pounded so hard it hurt, her lips tingling from Edward's kiss.

"We ought not to return to the ballroom together," he said as he backed into the dark hallway. "We will raise suspicion."

Grace nodded, unable to speak.

He smiled as he turned around, retreating into the hall without another word. He simply walked away, leaving Grace to sort through the torrent of emotions within her.

She brought her hand to her lips, leaning back against the wooden door. Her legs shook as she struggled to make sense of her racing thoughts. Among them, one thing was certain. That kiss had given her much to consider.

# Chapter 17

Edward had not seen Grace return to the ballroom all evening. He saw Mr. and Mrs. Weston usher their eldest daughter into the hall in search of her. Eventually he had seen the sweep of Grace's pastel yellow skirts as they passed the doorway, along with her family, in departure.

He spent the rest of the evening with his thoughts far from the party, but rather on how perfectly Grace had felt in his arms, how it had felt to kiss her. The warmth and softness of her lips would not desert his mind, the intensity of emotion her kiss had awakened within him. He had never experienced a kiss that affected him so greatly. He had been completely undone by her.

How could he wait the three days she required to make her decision? He didn't want a single day to pass without seeing her. He wanted to find her again tomorrow, gather

her up in his arms, and kiss her all over again, whether she planned to marry him or not.

On the ride home from Pengrave, Henry remained silent, apparently sensing Edward's deep contemplation. When they arrived at Clemsworth, their butler greeted them solemnly.

Henry stepped through the door first, removing his hat as the butler spoke in a hushed voice. "Lord Coventry requests your immediate presence," he said. The urgency in his tone sent a heavy stone of worry to settle in Edward's stomach.

He exchanged a look with Henry as they walked quickly toward their father's bedchamber. Edward stopped in the doorway first, his heart dropping as he saw his father, with his mother at his side, looking more grave than he had ever appeared before.

Edward stepped into the room, stopping at the foot of his father's bed.

"All my affairs are nearly complete," his father rasped. "But I thought it prudent to bid my two sons farewell. I will not live to see the sun rise."

Edward swallowed hard against the strange grief that gripped him.

His father's eyes found his. "Before it is too late I must confess something to both of you, especially Edward." His breath rattled. "I am pleased to have seen a change in you, Edward, witnessed by your mother on my behalf. Such changes I believed would require drastic measures to attain." His voice was slow and clipped, difficult to understand. "I did *attempt* to have my title and the estate of Clemsworth transferred to Henry, but the law would not allow it. After that, I chose a different plan. From the beginning, I confess, this disinheritance has been impossible."

Edward could not stop his jaw from dropping. Disbelief pounded in his skull. "You mean to say you tricked me?"

"Your mother desired that you marry, and I knew nothing short of a disinheritance could motivate you to such an endeavor. At my passing you will still assume my title and all properties aside from the estate promised to Henry in Worthing."

Edward laughed in disbelief. "How can this be true?"

He glanced at his mother to affirm the words his father had spoken. She stared at her husband in surprise, apparently oblivious to his scheme.

"Do you realize the torture you have forced me to endure? The heartache and desperation?" Anger rose in Edward's chest.

"And it has left you a changed man," his father said. "A more determined and focused one, I daresay. One who has found a purpose once more, who will run this estate and care well for my wife and daughter, and even a wife and children of his own." He paused to cough, the movement wracking his frail body.

Edward's mind spun. He thought of the days he had spent in desperate pursuit of a marriage with Grace. Still, he could not view the time as wasted. With his father's revelation, Edward examined his heart. He found that he still loved Grace, and he still wished to marry her. There was no question, no doubt. In a strange way, he was grateful his father had lied to him. If not, he would have never come to know Grace as he did.

"Thank you, father," Edward said, surprised by his own choice of words.

His father smiled, just a brief upturning of his mouth. A rare sight, the last smile Edward would ever see on his father's face.

Edward, Henry, and their mother waited in Lord Coventry's room until he died, a few short hours later. Juliet had already given her farewell and had been sent to bed, too young to witness death. In the early hours of the morning, Edward finally made his way to his bedchamber, dazed and too tired to think clearly. His father's death had struck him more deeply than he had expected.

As exhausted as he was, he found it difficult to sleep. His heart stung with grief, battling with the relief he felt at his father's trickery. Edward would keep his inheritance.

He had always thought it strange that his father had surpassed the laws of primogeniture. He should have realized it was nothing but a lie. He stared at the ceiling in the dark, processing the last several hours and all that had occurred, trying to understand the grief in his heart.

The next several days would be filled with burial preparations and mourning. He prepared himself for the gloom that awaited him—including the prospect that Grace's answer would come as another rejection.

But now he had the wealth she sought, the title, the property, all with certainty. Surely that was enough for her to accept him.

His heart ached as he finally drifted into a restless sleep.

# Chapter 18

The death of Lord Coventry came as little of a shock to the people of Brighton. All except for Grace.

When she had received the news three days before, she had spent much of the day in her bedchamber with guilt writhing in her stomach. Edward had not become engaged. That meant he would lose his inheritance, all because Grace had been too stubborn—too afraid. She wondered why she had not heard the gossip of his disinheritance. But of course, she had not ventured outside of the house in days.

Today, she lay on her bed with a book opened in front of her. Every time she attempted to read, the words spun off the page, becoming lost in the array of more important thoughts that begged for attention. She owed Edward her answer today. Her three days were spent. But since his father's death, he was no longer required to marry. Would he rescind his proposal? Surely he would. How could he even look upon her after she had caused him to lose his title and fortune?

The moment she had left the ball three nights before, she had made her decision.

She would marry him.

She would dare to trust him, a risk she hadn't been willing to take until that night. She had planned to tell him the next day, but his father had already died.

He would never have her now.

Harriett's voice came from the doorway, gentle and quiet. "Grace."

Her eyes lifted.

Harriett stood halfway in the room and half out, a smile on her lips. "There is someone here to see you."

Grace's heart leapt. She studied Harriett's face, searching for a clue of who it might be. Could it be Edward? The very idea set her hands shaking, the memory of their kiss still burning in her mind.

"Uncle Cornelius," Harriett said. "He wishes to speak with you."

Disappointment and relief dropped through her at once. Grace dragged herself to her feet, fixing the tie at her waist before venturing out the door. The air in the second floor hallway was clear and crisp, unlike the stuffy, hot air of her bedchamber. She descended the stairs, forcing a smile when she saw her uncle at the base, grinning as he always did.

When she reached him, her uncle gripped her fingers in his gloved hand. "Do not be angry with Harriett, but she has told me in great detail of your plight."

Grace shifted her gaze to her sister, who looked away guiltily.

"Uncle Cornelius can always be trusted," Harriett said. "You know this."

Her uncle cleared his throat, a pleased smile on his lips. "It does not require much intelligence at all to see that Lord Ramsbury is in love with you. At my dinner party he could scarcely keep his eyes away from you." Uncle Cornelius chuckled, leaning on his cane, one he carried strictly for fashionable purposes. "It doesn't matter that he has lost his inheritance. If he was in love with you before, he will be in love with you still. Love's not Time's fool," he said, quoting the very passage Edward had meant to share with her the day of his second proposal.

Grace smiled, her throat tight with emotion. "Love alters not with his brief hours and weeks, but bears it out, even to the edge of doom," she added in a soft voice. "Do you truly believe it?"

Her uncle nodded. "I loved my wife from the day I met her until the day she passed on." His eyes twinkled with something bright, hopeful, and lasting. Love.

"What do you suggest I do?"

"Find him, tell him you still wish to marry him. Your three days are nearly spent, are they not?"

Grace turned to Harriett, raising one eyebrow. "It seems you did tell him every detail."

She bit her lip. "I suppose I did."

Releasing a heavy breath, Grace rubbed her hands on her skirts, terror rising up her spine. "Perhaps... perhaps I may wait until tomorrow. This is a very difficult time for his family, and he will not wish to be interrupted. There are funeral services to be planned."

"Even more the reason for you to go today," her uncle said. "Give him a reason to smile, my dear."

She stared at the floor, her heart racing. "I cannot simply arrive on the front step of Clemsworth alone, intruding on their family during such a delicate time."

"Where else do you expect to find him?" Uncle Cornelius asked. "But if it will ease your fear, I will send your Aunt Christine to accompany you by coach."

Grace puzzled over the idea before slumping against the banister in a most unladylike fashion. "I am being absurd. I cannot go. He will never want me after I have caused him to lose so much. How could he?"

Her uncle's gentle demeanor shifted to one of severity, a look she had never seen cross his normally exuberant and smiling face. "You must go! Harriett and I will accompany you there if we must, won't we, Harriett?"

She nodded, a gleam of excitement in her eyes.

Grace struggled to breathe as she looked out the window, the distant sea visible under the morning sun. "Aunt Christine will suffice," she muttered.

Uncle Cornelius did not conceal his glee as he placed his hat atop his head. "I will fetch her now and return shortly." He disappeared through the door.

As promised, he arrived within minutes with a disgruntled Aunt Christine at his side. She fanned her face from the exertion of the swift walk. "If I am called upon to chaperone again I will be forced to take up a cane," she huffed.

Harriett squeezed Grace's arm, the last bit of encouragement she needed before her uncle ushered her into his coach, the one that had conveyed him here, and sent the coachman in the direction of Clemsworth. Grace's insides twisted with fear as they traveled, her gaze fixed out the window. What would she say to Edward? She practiced her words in her mind, but none of them seemed right, none eloquent enough to convey the message she intended to speak.

How inappropriate it would be to drop herself on the doorstep of Clemsworth, the estate she had caused Edward to never be allowed to call his own. Even with her aunt in tow it would be extremely rude to impose on the family during their grief.

Short minutes later, the coach stopped on the drive in front of Clemsworth. Grace stayed in her seat, trying to calm her breathing. Edward was expecting her today, she reminded herself. She had promised that she would tell him her decision. He wouldn't be surprised to see her, would he?

Aunt Christine crossed her arms over her ample chest, raising both brows into her cap. "Why are you delaying? I am not keen to stay in a hot coach all day. I am positively roasting," she said, withdrawing her fan again.

"I need just a moment to—" Grace looked out the window, shocked to see Edward walking across the neat lawn, straight toward her coach. Her heart jumped in her chest like a startled cat.

Aunt Christine slumped against her cushion, closing her eyes as she leaned her head back. "I will be here until you are finished. Mind your reputation, dear."

Grace hardly comprehended her aunt's suggestion. The coachman opened the door, offering his hand to let Grace out. Already she felt her face burning with shame. The beauty of Clemsworth had never struck her as much as it did now. It was as if the beautiful stone, immaculate gardens, and clear windows whispered to Grace of her cruelty for causing Edward to lose them.

When her feet touched the grass, she looked up. Edward had stopped in front of her, his expression surprising. She did not see hatred or malice, but only apprehension. He was dressed in mourning, the black a sharp contrast to his blue eyes.

She lowered her head in a bow of greeting, willing her cheeks to cool. What could she say to him? Nothing would be enough.

"I have been waiting for you to arrive," he said, drawing an audible breath. "Shall we take a walk around the gardens?"

Grace lifted her gaze, her brow contracting. Why did he wish to walk with her? On her way to Clemsworth she had prepared herself for the possibility that he would throw her off the property in anger. His eyes grew softer, more calm as he took her hand, guiding it to his elbow.

She gathered her composure, glancing up at him as they walked over the grounds toward the back property. She felt safe beside him, an overwhelming sense of belonging. She did not feel that he housed any anger toward her at all.

When they passed the back corner of the house, the gardens bloomed straight ahead, colorful and bright, giving her the courage to speak.

"I—I express my sincere condolences for your loss," she said, her voice weak and full of shame. The loss she spoke of implied more than his father's death. "How difficult it must be to lose your father and your living." She choked on a surge of guilt. How could she tell him now that she wished to marry him, when she could have told him before and prevented his second great loss? She couldn't do it.

He looked down at her, his expression unreadable.

She pressed her lips together to keep them from quivering. "It is my fault," she whispered. "My indecision has brought this fate upon you." She shook her head. "I cannot expect you to forgive me, and I cannot expect that your offer is still available to me… "

Without warning, he stopped walking as they passed a large hedge. His eyes stared into hers, careful, unyielding. "You would consider marrying me even without my inheritance?"

She inhaled deeply, seeking reassurance in his eyes. She realized with surprise that his offer still stood, visible in every line of his face, in the admiration and hope that burned there. "Yes," she breathed. Sudden tears stung her eyes. "I love you, Edward. And I am sorry, so very sorry. You have lost so much because of me." She dropped her hand from his arm, covering her face. "I have torn this beautiful home from you because of my indecision and stubbornness." She pressed her hands against her cheeks. "Where will we live?"

He pulled her hands away, staring down at her with a smile.

"What reason could you have to smile at a time like this?" She scowled as tears hovered on her lower lashes.

He leaned down and kissed her, causing her frustration to melt as his arms wrapped around her waist. His mouth moved over hers, fervent and slow. "You said we," he whispered, half against her lips as he kissed her again, his fingers threading in her hair. Grace clung to him, setting aside her confusion for the moment. She laughed amid her tears, pulling him closer, kissing him with all the energy she possessed. She did not care where they would live, only that they would be together.

He pulled back, just enough to speak. "We will live here, at Clemsworth," he murmured. His lips moved to her cheek, her forehead, his mouth melting into a smile amid his kisses.

It took all of her concentration to recall his words. She clutched his face, pulling back enough to see his eyes.

"Here?" she exclaimed.

His smile widened. "My father's stipulation was all trickery. He could not surpass the laws that bound me to my inheritance."

She stared at him in shock. "What could have compelled him to do that?"

"He wished to see me married, believing a woman would help me change, improve somehow. He thought his threatening to disinherit me the only way to achieve his designs." Edward smiled. "I believe he was right. You have changed me, Grace. I meant to tell you of my father's trickery when you first arrived, but… I wished to see what your answer would be without knowing—if you would desire to marry me without my possessions."

Relief flooded through her. "You cannot be serious."

"I am most serious."

Her heart soared, but a question still burned inside her. "Are you certain you still wish to marry me? It is no longer required of you."

He tipped his head back with an exasperated sigh. "Yes, for what must be the tenth time." He gave her a teasing smile, bending down to steal another kiss from her, as if he could not help it. "I love you, and I always shall. Only you, Grace."

She smiled without reservation, hope and peace pulsing through her body like a song. He took her hand in his, setting out along the garden path once again. "Our engagement will bring a much needed gladness to Clemsworth. My mother and Juliet will be so pleased. Even Henry, though he doubted you would ever agree to marry me."

"I doubted it myself."

Edward chuckled. "You never did allow me to quote the sonnet I meant to share with you on my second proposal." He smiled down at her, a mischievous gleam in his eyes.

She raised her brows. "You may do so now if you wish."

He grinned, clearing his throat. "Let me not to the marriage of two minds," he said, his voice loud and elaborate. "Love is not love, which alters when it alteration finds, or—"

"*True*. Let me not to the marriage of *true* minds," she corrected.

He scoffed. "Well, if I had been the one to write it, it would have been written differently."

"I see your pride has returned."

"As have your snide remarks."

She smiled. "They will never be in short supply as long as you are married to me. Nor will my well-delivered insults."

He concealed his grin, rubbing his jaw. "I wonder if Miss Reed would like to marry me instead. Miss Darby, perhaps? Surely they will not insult me."

Grace gasped, leading Edward to bend over in laughter as they mounted the front steps. "You are insufferable." A smile broke through her act of annoyance, his expression all too endearing. She did not know how she had ever doubted him. All her uncertainty had fled, replaced with the warm understanding that she was loved. And that was all she would ever need.

Edward gave another of his charming smiles. "I am insufferable? That is a dreadful thing to say to your betrothed."

"Very well. I find you barely tolerable."

He laughed, covering her hand with both of his, enveloping it in warmth and strength. "Now I know you are only pretending."

# Epilogue

Leaves of every warm color crunched under Juliet's feet as she ran across the front lawn of Clemsworth. Autumn had come early to Brighton, filling the air with a chill and greeting the trees with colors of contrasting warmth.

Grace stood on the front steps, wrapped in a cloak, her husband's arm around her. They had been married for nearly four months, and Grace counted them as the best four months of her life. They laughed as Juliet threw a handful of leaves into the air beneath a distant tree on the property, spinning as they fell all around her.

Edward's voice vibrated against Grace as he called out to his sister, "You must spin faster. Try to achieve five rotations before the first leaf touches the ground."

Juliet nodded with enthusiasm, scooping up another handful of leaves. Grace peeked up at Edward, placing a kiss on the corner of his jaw, calling his eyes to hers. "You always seem to have a new idea to entertain her." She smiled. "Fortunately, Juliet is easily entertained."

He grinned. "I suspect you were easily entertained as a child. But not with activities such as this. You were always with a book."

Grace raised a scolding finger. "Do not tell me it is not a worthy way to spend one's time. If not for my extensive reading I would never have determined that Mr. Harrison was the perfect match for Harriett." Releasing a heavy sigh, Grace stared up at the clouds. "He will return to Brighton any day now, and Harriett will begin falling in love with him."

Edward chuckled, tucking his arm tighter around her waist. "How can you be so certain?"

"I have a sense for these things."

He kissed the top of her head, laughing into her hair. "If that is so, then why did you take so long to *sense* that I was in love with you?"

She shrugged. "You do have a way of leaving me rather senseless."

"Oh?" He stared down at her as if he had just been offered a challenge. And Grace knew he never could resist a challenge. Nudging his fingers under her chin, he lowered his lips to hers, stealing her breath and words and all coherent thought. He wrapped both arms around her waist, lifting her off the porch in a circle. She laughed as he kissed her again, her feet floating above the stone steps, a thrilling and rather *senseless* experience.

When Edward set her down, his cold hand wrapped around hers, the chilled autumn air turning his cheeks and the tip of his nose pink. "I have a rather special tea tray prepared for us today," he said.

Grace narrowed her eyes, sensing a surprise behind

his words. His lips lifted in a grin as he pulled her toward the door.

When Juliet had been called inside, they made their way to the drawing room, where the hearth burned bright and a tea tray sat covered by a silver lid on the coffee table. Edward's mother, the Dowager Countess of Coventry, awaited with her knitting, positioned on a nearby armchair with a smile.

Edward led Grace to the sofa before lifting the lid, revealing a plate of fresh Shrewsbury cakes. The scent of butter and lemon wafted up to her nose.

She gasped in delight, leaping to her feet to kiss her husband's cheek. She blushed, remembering the presence of both her mother and sister-in-law. Juliet giggled, reaching eagerly to claim the first cake.

Edward smiled as Grace reclaimed her seat, resuming her duty as hostess by pouring tea. She shared a glance with her husband as she set down the teapot, conveying her gratitude with her eyes as she took a bite of her cake, the sweet gift Edward had given her.

He settled into the sofa beside her, taking her hand once again.

She knew, as much as she knew the Shrewsbury cakes of Brighton could never be improved upon—as much as she knew Harriett and Mr. William Harrison were the perfect match—that she and Edward were the perfect match as well.

She gripped his hand tighter, listening to his laughter, counting it as her greatest gift of all.

# Find the complete series on Amazon

Brides of Brighton
A CONVENIENT ENGAGEMENT
MARRYING MISS MILTON
ROMANCING LORD RAMSBURY
MISS WESTON'S WAGER
AN UNEXPECTED BRIDE

# About the Author

Ashtyn Newbold grew up with a love of stories. When she discovered chick flicks and Jane Austen books in high school, she learned she was a sucker for romantic ones. When not indulging in sweet romantic comedies and regency period novels (and cookies), she writes romantic stories of her own across several genres. Ashtyn also enjoys baking, singing, sewing, and anything that involves creativity and imagination.

www.ashtynnewbold.com

Printed in Great Britain
by Amazon